Bold Journey

A Novel by
Charles Bohner

BOLD
JOURNEY

WEST WITH LEWIS AND CLARK

HOUGHTON MIFFLIN COMPANY   BOSTON   1985

Library of Congress Cataloging in Publication Data

Bohner, Charles H.
  Bold journey.

  Summary: Private Hugh McNeal relates his experiences
accompanying Captains Lewis and Clark on their 1804–1806
expedition in search of a northwest passage to the Pacific
Ocean.
  1. Lewis and Clark Expedition (1804–1806)—Juvenile
fiction. [1. Lewis and Clark Expedition (1804–1806)—
Fiction. 2. West (U.S.)—Discovery and exploration—
Fiction. 3. Frontier and pioneer life—Fiction.
4. Voyages and travels—Fiction] I. Title.
PZ7.B63583Bo 1985   [Fic]   84-19328
ISBN 0-395-36691-7

For Russell

Author's Note

Although much is known of the Lewis and Clark Expedition of 1804–1806, almost nothing is known of Private Hugh McNeal, one of the young men who went with the two captains in search of a northwest passage to the Pacific Ocean. He enlisted, he survived, and he was paid for his services by a grateful government. His name appears here and there in the accounts of the exploration, but otherwise history is silent. I have tried in this book to imagine the part that he may have played, and I have allowed him to describe his reactions to the Native Americans he was encountering for the first time in the words of a man of his own times. The adventures of Hugh McNeal that follow are fiction, but his story is as true to the record and to the spirit of that remarkable journey as I have been able to make it.

C.B.

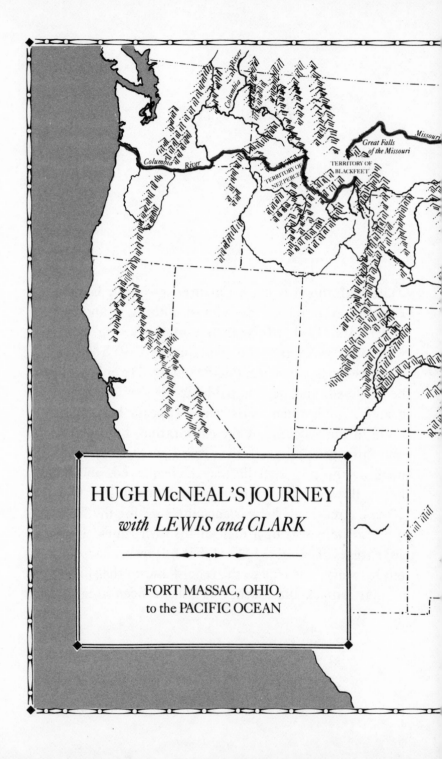

Columbia River

Columbia River

Great Falls
of the Missouri

Missouri

TERRITORY OF
NEZ PERCE

TERRITORY OF
BLACKFEET

HUGH McNEAL'S JOURNEY

with LEWIS and CLARK

FORT MASSAC, OHIO,
to the PACIFIC OCEAN

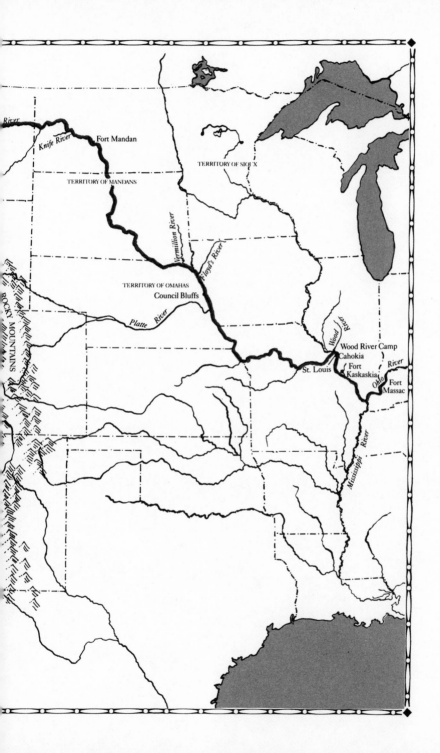

Contents

Bold Journey

Strangers from Upstream

If I had known how cursed and lonesome and God-forsaken life was in President Jefferson's Army, I would never have joined up. They sent me at once to Fort Massac, a swampy, flea-bit outpost on the Ohio River about three days' march from where it joins the Mississippi. Squeezed by the river on the south and choked by the forest on the north, we fought mainly the ticks and the mosquitoes. At that time and in that section they were bolder and more troublesome than either the French or the Indians.

Jack Newman and I were splitting wood outside the stockade. We had spent the night on guard duty, and our last chore before getting some grub and some sleep was to fill Captain Bissell's wood box. When enough logs were split to warm the officers, we could go back and shiver around our own campfires.

We had stopped to catch our breath. Jack was searching his pockets for tobacco, and I was sitting on a stump thinking of breakfast. Suddenly I felt a chill strike my marrow, not just the chill of a damp November morning but the chill of a forest come alive with shrieks and shadows. Those who have lived long in the wilderness will know what I mean. Something, I didn't know what, made me reach for my rifle.

Jack put up his hand.

"It's Drewyer," he said.

Jack was right. George Drewyer had been peering at us from the dark green shade. Now he strode lightly into the clearing, moving silently in his moccasins. Four geese dripping blood hung over his shoulder. Drewyer was a crack shot.

"There is no danger," he said. "Dahn-zher," he pronounced it in his French accent. Then he laughed.

His was a sneering laugh, full of contempt for a soldier's life, a life of standing guard and taking orders and chopping wood for officers. George Drewyer was not a soldier and he would never be one. We all wondered what exactly was his tie to the Army of the Frontier. He would vanish into the forest for weeks at a time and then reappear as abruptly as he did that morning, his face hidden behind a bushy beard and his squinty, restless eyes seeing everything and telling nothing.

He sat down on a stump, dropped the geese at his feet, and pulled out a twist of tobacco. He didn't offer any to us.

"Whose boats?"

Drewyer nodded in the direction of the river bank, where a keelboat and two pirogues, one red and one white, were tied up under the bluff of the fort.

"I don't know," I said.

Drewyer snickered. *"Mon Dieu!* You call yourself a guard?"

I started to explain that they had arrived last night while I was at supper, but Jack Newman cut in. "They came downriver last evening," he said. "About twenty men."

"And two captains," Drewyer added.

We both swung around and stared at him in surprise.

"Two captains," he repeated. "One dark, one redheaded."

"If you knew, why'd you ask?" Jack said, a little hotly.

Paying Jack no mind, Drewyer got up and slung the geese over his shoulder.

"They are fools to go downriver at low water," he said. *"Imbéciles!* You can see they are not watermen."

"Where are they going?" I asked.

He started to walk away without answering, then stopped and looked back over his shoulder.

He stared at me for a moment as if deciding whether to answer. Finally he said, "They go to the Pacific Ocean."

Before Jack and I could take in that amazing

news, he had vanished into the forest as suddenly and silently as he had come.

Well, I got to wondering about those strangers. So as soon as that pesky wood box was filled, I scrambled down the yellow mud banks to the river to have a look for myself. That keelboat tied up under the bluffs might have done for floating logs down to New Orleans, but it was fit for little else. It was a clumsy effort, about fifty feet long, top-heavy in the cabin and swollen in the middle like a rotten catfish. You don't grow up on the banks of the Ohio River without becoming a judge of river craft. That keelboat was nothing for style.

At the stern a man was sitting over a map that he had spread out on the deck. The morning fog still hung over the river, and he had pulled a buffalo robe close about his shoulders against the chill. He looked pale and feverish to me. I guessed he had come down with the party, although he wasn't in uniform.

When he looked up, I called out to him, "I'll come on board and look her over."

He studied me for a moment. At last he said, very slowly, "You will not!" and turned back to his map.

That nettled me. I took a turn up and down the bank to have a better look. He pretended not to see me and bent lower over his map.

"She's riding sort of low," I said.

When he didn't answer or look up, I added, "She's loaded all wrong."

That ruffled his feathers, and his head jerked up from the map.

"What do you mean, she's loaded wrong?"

"Just what I said. She wants more weight in the bow. That way, if you ride up on a sandbar, you can easy back her off. But if you slide up onto one with your stern lagging like she is, you'll be there until spring freshet."

I watched him turn that over in his mind. He was one of the quality, and he didn't want to be told anything by the likes of me. But he had the sense to see that I was right. He looked poorly, a sallow face and sunken eyes. I wasn't feeling much better myself, what with lack of sleep and lack of breakfast, so I spread myself a little more. "She's too squat, anyhow, for these waters," I said.

At that he stood up, not very steadily, and I wondered whether he wasn't so much sick as drunk. He pulled his robe around his shoulders and pointed down to the pirogues.

"What's your considered opinion of them?" he asked.

You could find a pirogue anywhere on the river in those days. Nowadays you'd call them dugout canoes. You took a log of sycamore or cottonwood and hollowed it out by fire, then smoothed down the inside with an adz.

"Not bad," I allowed. "Not good either." I shrugged my shoulders.

"You're smart as paint," he said.

"I can tell a keelboat from a hog trough," I said.

He looked up and down his boat as if, against his will, he half agreed with me.

The stranger didn't say anything more. Instead, he carefully folded his map and started to step down into the cabin. Before his head disappeared below, he looked at me with those troubled eyes and said, none too friendly, "You! Keep off this boat!"

"She's loaded all wrong," I hollered after him, just for devilment, but he let on he hadn't heard.

If I'd known who I was talking to that morning, I would have kept my mouth shut. It would have been better for me.

A Redheaded Captain

The stranger on the keelboat was maybe twenty-five or a little more. I reckoned he was from Virginia. He was touchy, the way so many of them are back there, sort of stiff-necked and snarly. It did me good to cross him; perked up my morning. I started to clamber back up the bank to the fort, feeling much improved. Halfway up I heard Jack Newman shouting to me. He was standing at the gate and waving his arms.

Jack and I had enlisted at the same time and been sent to the frontier. He was from Philadelphia and he never let you forget it. When I told him I was from Wheeling, he said that was the wild West, which I suppose it was. Jack was smart, book-smart, and had a quick tongue. He could answer up to the officers in a way the rest of us envied. If you had shot a squirrel at fifty paces, Jack had shot one at a hundred. If you had visited Pittsburgh, he had visited Boston. We had nothing in common but homesickness and boredom, but in the Army that was enough to make us friends.

"Where've you been?" Jack asked as I came up.

"Looking over those boats."

"You better hump yourself. Captain Bissell's looking for you."

"What for?"

Jack shook his head. If he knew, he wouldn't tell. He was a queer fish, no doubt about it.

I hurried across the parade ground to Captain Bissell's log hut and knocked on the door. When he shouted for me to come in, I stepped inside, closed the door, and pulled myself to attention. I was a little out of breath.

Captain Bissell was standing with a stranger before a roaring fire. They had their backs to the blaze, and coming in out of the sunlight I had trouble making out their faces. The room was boiling hot, probably with the wood I'd chopped.

Captain Bissell said, "Here is the man I've been telling you about."

It surprised me a little that Captain Bissell even knew my name.

The stranger looked me over.

"You're Private Hugh McNeal?"

I allowed as how I was.

The stranger was tall, at least a head taller than I was, with bright red hair and the rusty, mottled skin that goes with it.

"I am here on orders direct from President Jefferson," he said.

That sounds a little highfalutin now that I tell it, but that's what he said. And he said it in the no-nonsense way of a man who says it because it's a fact and who favors facts. Maybe he did lead up to it a little more, not just spring it out that way. If he did, I forget it now.

I glanced over at Captain Bissell, and he nodded.

"I'm looking for men," the stranger said. "I aim to recruit a party to go up the Missouri River. We're to explore its banks and those of the Columbia River. We expect to find the Northwest Passage to the Pacific Ocean."

The Northwest Passage! My father, who was a boat-builder at Wheeling, would talk endlessly about it. It was the great topic of everybody on the river. To fill the hours of fashioning keels and ribs, they would speculate on the places their boats might go and the cargo of wealth and wonders to be brought back. I've seen them shout in each other's faces and come to blows over the depths of the Western rivers and the heights of the mountains that blocked the way to the Pacific Ocean.

And here was this redhead saying so matter-of-factly that he intended to go out there and find it himself. Not only that. He gave you the feeling that if it could be found, he was the man to find it.

"Do you know what I'm talking about?" the stranger asked.

I said yes, I knew about the Northwest Passage.

"It's a task," he continued, "for men who know the wilderness. We'll have only what we can carry with us. We'll go where no white man has gone before. There'll be Sioux, Blackfeet, and God knows what others. We may find" — and here he smiled — "that the savages have ways of making us feel unwelcome."

This speech, which he must have made many times in the course of collecting his party, was delivered in the dry, flat accents of Kentucky. The stranger was, in fact, a pretty fair specimen of Kentucky, all slabs and angles, his moving parts a little loose in the sockets.

He stood there watching me, and I felt behind him the eyes of Captain Bissell.

"Why are you telling all this to me?" I asked him.

"We've got interpreters," he said. "We've got woodsmen and trappers. What we need now are watermen, men who know the rivers, who can shoot rapids, who can sail and portage. There are not many such in the Army. Captain Bissell tells me that you're such a person. Are you?"

"I know the river."

"Can you repair boats?"

"Pretty well," I said.

I was glad my pa wasn't there to hear me say

that. After years of trying to teach me, he'd told me to go join the Army.

"Very well, then. Will you come?"

The stranger waited, his red hair shining in the firelight and his clear eyes taking my measure. Suddenly it hit me that I was to decide then and there. Just like that!

I don't know what possessed me. Who would choose in a moment to trade the easy life in a fort for the risks of being crushed by a grizzly bear or scalped by a howling savage? But something about that stranger, his readiness to take on anything, made you want to have his good opinion. And I was, after all, eighteen years old and didn't know any better.

When I didn't answer at once, the stranger said, "I guess you're wondering what it pays?"

"Is it more than I get now?"

He and Captain Bissell looked at each other.

"First, six months' pay," he said, "in advance. And when we return, as much land in the West as the government gave to the men who served in the War of Independence."

"Four hundred acres?"

"You know that?"

I nodded. I knew that. My pa had served for three years on the frontier with General George Rogers Clark. Pa had got his land as promised, and I often heard him curse himself for selling it for ready money.

"I'll go," I said.

"Good."

He started to turn away, and I understood that I was dismissed, when suddenly he turned back as if he had forgotten one detail.

"My name," he said, "is Captain William Clark."

The name meant nothing to me. Only later did I learn that he was the youngest brother of my father's old commanding officer, and that he had five older brothers who had fought in the War for Independence.

"Be ready at seven tomorrow morning," he said. "We'll leave then."

"Then you'll leave in the fog, Captain," I said.

He shot me a glance. "What time does it lift?"

"Not before eight."

"Eight!"

"At least eight. Maybe later."

"Then we'll leave at eight."

Captain Clark looked over at Captain Bissell. "By tomorrow morning," he said, "we'll know if Private McNeal is a waterman."

I saluted, turned, and stepped back into the sunlight. I had joined the Corps of Discovery, made the choice with no more thought than you'd give to tossing down a whiskey punch on a frosty night.

❧ 3 ❧
The Corps of Discovery

Lucky for me the fog the next morning was as heavy and sticky as wet flannel. Not that Captain Clark needed me to warn him about the Ohio River in low water. The sandbars lay in wait like Sioux warriors. Sometimes you could spot a sandbar, the riffle of breaking water telling anybody with one eye to stand clear. Worse mischief was done by the snags, tree trunks that lurked just below the surface, sawing up and down in the current and waiting to poke a rib out of your keelboat when it was least convenient. The lows that year, 1803, were unnatural, November being always the lowest month anyway.

I judged that, fog or no fog, Captain Clark expected me at the boats by seven, so I took care to be there at the proper time, packed and ready. Soldiers were already moving about dimly in the mist, and a half-dozen rough-looking Frenchmen were sitting around a fire drinking hot rum.

The keelboat was leaking, and several men had

been set to bailing her. I hadn't noticed the day before that a mast could be stepped amidships. Three men were busy raising it and setting a large square sail. The breeze was already stirring out of the southeast, and I guessed we would be sailing.

I heard somebody shouting, "McNeal." Looking up the bluff toward the fort, I saw Jack Newman making his way toward me, slipping and staggering under a heavy pack.

"Did you think you were leaving without me?" he asked.

My heart sank to see him.

"What are you doing here?" I asked, although the reason was clear enough.

"Going exploring," he said, "just like you."

I had only to look into that grinning face to discover that a lot of my pleasure at being picked was based on the fact that Jack had been passed over.

"When did Captain Clark talk to you?" I asked.

"Before he talked to you."

"Why didn't you tell me what was in the wind?"

"Why didn't you ask me? I notice that you were quiet enough about it."

Captain Clark must have heard Jack bawling my name, for he stuck his head out of the forecastle of the keelboat and looked around.

"You two," he called. "Come on board."

He watched us climb up onto the deck.

"Find an empty locker for your packs," he said. "Then you can lend a hand bailing."

We had to lift the lids of a dozen lockers before we found an empty one. The keelboat was already laden to the gunwales, and the lockers were stuffed with goods mostly labeled PHILADELPHIA. Jack said he recognized the names of some of the traders, and maybe he was telling the truth. If the rest of the boat was as badly made as those lockers, we were in for a long trip. The planks were already warped and the fittings were coming loose.

Jack and I fell to bailing, as ordered. Jack began at once to complain. "If this is exploring, give me guard duty."

Bailing was all right with me. The keelboat had places for twenty-two oars. We'd be going downstream until we reached the Mississippi, but from then on it was upstream all the way to the Pacific Ocean. More than once I had pulled an oar of a fully loaded keelboat, and Jack had not. I figured I'd enjoy the bailing while I could.

We heard someone laughing, and there standing in the doorway of the cabin was George Drewyer, finishing his breakfast. He gnawed the last piece of flesh off a bone, flung it into the river, and wiped his beard with the back of his hand. He commenced picking his black, snaggled teeth with a long, dirty fingernail.

"So," he said, "you two are going. I feel less danger."

I fell to bailing, but Jack said, "Why shouldn't we go? There's money to be made."

"Money? You go for money?"

Jack didn't answer but threw a bucket of bilge water into the river.

Drewyer reached into his shirt, pulled out something, and thrust it into Jack's face.

"Regard," Drewyer said in his French accent. "How much money for this?"

I stopped bailing to get a closer look.

Drewyer held it up before us, dangling it by the fur or the hair and letting it swing slowly back and forth before our eyes.

Jack reached for it, but Drewyer snatched it back.

"No!" he snapped.

"What is it?" I asked.

Drewyer smiled. "The scalp of a white woman," he said.

I felt my blood run cold. Some savage, his tomahawk slick with blood, had torn it from a corpse still warm with life. It looked to me like the pelt of some small and timid animal, brown and skimpy.

George Drewyer stood there examining it curiously, and then he put it back carefully inside his leather shirt.

"It is interesting," he said. "You wish to go to the West." He patted his shirt where the scalp was hidden away. "*That* is the West."

"Are you trying to scare me?" Jack said. "It won't work."

Drewyer nodded his head knowingly and shook with his inward chuckle.

We turned back to our bailing. I couldn't stop thinking about that scalp. I'd never seen one before. I thrust my hand deep into the water and rubbed my fingers against my palm, as if the blood and gore from the scalp clung to me.

Jack put his head back and sniffed the air. "That Drewyer," he said. "He's ripe. I'd as soon be downwind a hog pen as George Drewyer."

Jack had grit. That scalp didn't seem to bother him at all.

I caught sight of Captain Clark standing up forward and watching us intently. Beside him was a man in a blue uniform coat with the two epaulettes of an Army captain on his shoulders.

Captain Clark signaled for us to join them. As we came up, I recognized the other captain as the man in buckskins who had been reading the map and had told me to keep clear of the keelboat.

"These are the two recruits from Fort Massac," Captain Clark said. He pointed a long forefinger at Newman and at me and pronounced our names.

We stood in front of this other captain and he looked us over as though we were cattle at an auction. He was shorter than Captain Clark and not nearly as well made. He was ramrod-stiff, and the tight fit of the jacket made him more so. It was, I saw, a really fancy coat, frosted with lace and glistening with brass buttons. It must have been made for him back east.

When he had finished inspecting us, he said, "Captain Clark, I am sure, has told you what you need to know. This is still the Army. Keep that in mind!"

I thought he looked hard at me when he made that last remark. If he remembered me from yesterday, he didn't let on. And I was in no haste to remind him that we had met before.

"Return to your bailing," he ordered.

When we got back, I said to Jack, "Who was that?"

Jack gave me a look as if I had lost my wits.

"Who was that?" he echoed. "You clodpole! That's Captain Meriwether Lewis!"

"Who's Meriwether Lewis?"

Jack's eyes bulged in his head.

"Well, don't that beat all," he said. "You flathead! He's kin to President Jefferson, was his private secretary. He's drunk champagne out of gold goblets with ambassadors and such like in Washington. He's in charge of this expedition."

"I never heard of him," I said.

"Well, you're from Wheeling," Jack said. "What do you expect?"

Meriwether Lewis didn't add up to my idea of an explorer. Standing so stiff and bandy-legged in his blue dress uniform, he looked to me like a parade-ground dandy. His face, moreover, was as unlined as a boy's. Only the eyes were old. Deep-set and dark and searching, those eyes have troubled my sleep more than once. When, years later, I picked up a month-old newspaper in a tavern and learned that Captain Meriwether Lewis was dead, I saw in my memory, I *felt*, those cold, haunted eyes.

❧ 4 ❧

Downstream to the Mississippi

We cast off as soon as the fog lifted. Captain Bissell had come down to the river edge. There was a flurry of handshaking between him and my new captains. As we swung out into the current, a cannon thundered a final salute from Fort Massac. Captain Lewis jumped up on the roof of the forecastle and began rapping out orders pretty smartly. I noticed that Captain Clark let him have his head about the boats. I wasn't overly keen on trying to serve two masters, and I was a little curious to see how we would all get on.

Jack Newman was ordered to row in one of the pirogues with the Frenchmen.

"What do you have to do?" he wanted to know.

I said I hadn't got any orders yet. I guessed I would be set to sailing, but I figured I'd let Jack find that out on his own.

"Don't you have to row, too?" he demanded.

"I don't know, I told you."

He gave me a suspicious look. "What did you tell Clark you can do?"

"I reckon he knows why he picked me," I said.

Jack gave me a hard look and skulked off.

Captain Lewis had changed his fancy blue coat for buckskin. I heard him ask Captain Clark which one of the new recruits was boat-savvy, and Captain Clark answered, "The Irishman." That was me and no mistake. My father was from County Antrim, and like him I had the map of Ireland on my face.

"You can set a square sail, can you?" Captain Lewis asked me. "If you can't," he added dryly, "I guess you can row."

I took hold of the two lines that held the lower corners of the sail and got my feet braced against a thwart. The breeze was rising with the sun, a wind honed and whetted by November weather.

It was as easy as falling down to handle one of those square sails on a keelboat once you had the knack of it. Mostly it was like flying a kite. When the wind freshened and the gusts came, you pulled the corners of the sail down flat and felt her leap ahead. Otherwise, you eased off and let what wind there was draw you along. We were getting into deeper water and the river was widening out, so we went booming along downstream.

That keelboat rolled and pitched on account of her cabins being too high, as I said before, but some of that I could counter with the sail. Higher up the Ohio it was too bendy for real sailing, but we had hit a straight stretch and could make headway. The men on board were glad enough to watch me sail her, for otherwise they'd be dipping oars. They were sitting on the lockers and Captain Clark was showing them how to weave heavy ropes out of elk skins.

I could feel Captain Lewis's eyes boring right into my back. But I had sailed for better skippers than any Army captain, so I put him out of mind. After a time he got busy with other things, and I reckoned he was content. The winter sky was burned off by the sun, and across the water I could see Jack sweating in the pirogue. Those pirogues skittered over the surface like spiders. The Frenchers sank the oars deep into the water, often raising themselves out of their seats as they heaved. They hollered and sang and every once in a while one of them would let out a whoop just for sheer cussedness.

About noon the breeze began to slacken, and I thought Captain Lewis would drop sail and turn out the rowers on the keelboat. But we were moving and he was willing to let her barrel along with the current. Since the sail was limp, I thought I would walk back to see how she handled. The steersman offered me a twist of tobacco.

"Looks like you done that afore," he said. "What's your name?"

"Hugh McNeal."

"You enlist at Fort Massac?"

"At Wheeling. They sent me to Massac."

"That so? I'm from Frankfort. Charley Floyd."

Charley wasn't much older than I was. His hair was so pale that it looked like down. Only by dint of effort and prayer had he raised a crop on his upper lip for a scraggly mustache. With his free hand he was pulling a droopy corner, as if to encourage it. The other hand grasped the end of the steering oar, which was locked under his arm. The oar was jouncing some and giving him fits.

"How does she handle?"

Charley looked around before he answered.

At last he said, "Leaves something to be desired."

"She's top-heavy," I said. "That's her trouble."

"You think so?"

"Don't you?"

He took another survey, and then bobbed his head in a quick nod of agreement.

"That's what I told Captain Lewis."

Charley's pale eyes narrowed. They looked naked, his eyelashes were so light. He said very slowly, "You told Captain Lewis?"

"Why not tell him? Shouldn't he know if he's got a tub for a boat?"

Charley sent a stream of tobacco juice to starboard and gave a thoughtful pull on his yellow mustache.

"Well, you see," Charley said, and he gave another tug, "Captain Lewis, he designed this keel-boat hisself."

"What?"

"Yup. Had her built up in Pittsburgh. Some might say he miscalculated. The man he got to build it for him turned out to have one powerful thirst. And you might add that Captain Lewis spent the summer keeping him sober and on the job. I reckon it didn't do much for the captain's temper, your telling him."

"I get your drift."

"Some people," Charley added, "might have kept them defects to themselves. The captain is a mite touchy on the subject."

I was turning that advice over in my mind when suddenly I heard a shout from the bow.

"You there!"

There was a slight chance it might not be me, so I kept looking astern.

"You! You there!"

Since the uproar was considerable, I thought I'd better turn around.

Captain Lewis was standing in the door of the cabin, his eyes burning and his face scarlet. He seemed to have got back his health.

"What are you doing?" he roared at me.

Since I was just at that point doing nothing at all, I decided not to testify.

He stepped out on deck and made his way to the mast.

"Didn't I order you to tend this sail?"

I tried to answer, but the words gagged in my throat.

"What did you say?"

This time I got them out. "Yes, sir!"

"Then why aren't you doing it?"

I looked around and shrugged my shoulders. "There's no wind," I said, then added a shade too late, "sir!"

His face got, if possible, a few shades darker. His mouth was working violently, but no words came out. He grabbed the rope I had lashed to the gunwale and shook it in a passion until the mast creaked in protest.

"Get up here!" he shouted. "And next time stay where I order you to stay."

I started forward.

"Move!" he shouted. "Faster!"

I hopped forward as fast as I could.

Captain Lewis started below. A lurch of the keelboat caught him and knocked him against the jamb. That was unlucky — for me. He stood there a moment, breathing hard.

"To spur your memory," he said over his shoulder, "you stand guard tonight. All night, soldier."

I hurried forward and grasped the lines of the sail.

The men on board were bending over their work as if they had just discovered that weaving elk ropes was as delicate as repairing clocks. I felt foolish enough, standing there in the silence. I caught a glimpse of Charley Floyd, but his pale eyes were fixed on some point far downstream. He hung on to the steering oar as if he half expected Captain Lewis's squall to throw up waves and swamp us.

Like a fool I had traded the easygoing Captain Bissell for this bandy-legged bantam cock. I looked over the gunwale at the Ohio rolling by. I was a strong swimmer. I just had to wait for a bend that would carry us close to shore. In a moment I could dive over, swim to shore, and disappear into the forest that grew down to the edge of the water. It was a new country and a big one. I could choose a new name, find a new home, and make a new life. Only one thing was holding me back. The Army shot deserters on sight. So I judged I'd give Captain Lewis a little more time before taking the dive.

I was on my way that night to stand guard when I heard a voice.

"*Mon Dieu!* You call yourself a guard?"

I turned around. It was Jack Newman.

"I will feel less dahn-ZHER," he said in a fair imitation of George Drewyer.

Then he broke out in loud, coarse laughter.

5

Volunteers for the West

Take a look at a map of the West and you can see the Ohio River beginning high up at Pittsburgh and snaking down to the place where it joins the Mississippi, more than a thousand miles below. The boat-builders up there in Pittsburgh had bamboozled Captain Meriwether Lewis, had told him that he'd never find a builder farther down the river. He believed it, swallowing the lie like any greenhorn. If he had made his way as far as Wheeling, my father might have built his keelboat for him. For the government's money Captain Lewis would have got a better boat than the leaky bucket he settled for.

And wouldn't my pa have crowed! He would as soon have one of his boats go on such a famous journey as one of his sons. He was a prideful man and built his boats with sweat and blood. He would speculate about the whereabouts of his favorites as if they were his children. I have seen him throw

down his tools and hurry off to the wharf when one
of his own reappeared like the prodigal son out of
the morning mists.

He was often in my thoughts as we began the run
downriver from Fort Massac. We had two days
of sailing downstream with fair winds and clear
weather until we reached the Mississippi. We all
let out a cheer when we came in sight of the point,
but we'd have been a mite less cheerful if we'd
considered what was in store for us. For we were
heading north, and north meant heading upstream,
and heading upstream meant rowing. And we
weren't going up one of your narrow, feeble, trickly
streams. We were breasting the Mississippi itself.
It was a sight to remember, the first glimpse of
that wide sheet of slate-gray water sliding calm
and silent and merciless round the bend.

We turned our bows into the current, making
slow progress against that mighty river. By now it
was almost December, and the winds came roaring
out of the northwest. We had to battle river and
sky, both of them gray and greasy as pewter. In
the morning the ground would be dusted with
snow, and we counted it a lucky day if we saw the
sun. My back and shoulders ached with the ever-
lasting rowing, and by evening the lines in the
palms of my hands were crusted with dried blood.
Rowing at least warmed your body, but your feet
stung with the cold and the wet. I hadn't been
really warm since Fort Massac. We were heading

for Fort Kaskaskia, several days' pull up the
Mississippi.

Everything was made worse by Jack Newman.
Nothing suited him. Worst of all, he stuck to me
like tar. Charley Floyd and I rowed side by side
in the keelboat and took turns at the steering oar.
Captain Lewis kept Jack in the red pirogue with
the Frenchmen, and that drove him wild.

Those Frenchmen were a hard lot. Most of them
had lived among the Indians and had picked up
savage ways. The biggest of them, La Liberté, a
burly, hairy scoundrel, had only a reddish blur
where his right eye once was. When he got drunk,
which was often, he would pull open the puckered
slit and thrust his face into yours, staggering about
and laughing crazily. Those rascals drove sharp
knuckles into Jack's back, and an occasional well-
aimed stroke of the blade sent a sheet of icy water
over him.

"Lewis did it on purpose," Jack complained.
"He took a dislike to me the first day."

We had built up our campfires against the damp
and the darkness. In the firelight Jack's face looked
pinched and angry.

"He's a slaveowner," Jack said. "High and
mighty. He's used to ordering black men. Well,
I'm a soldier but I'm not a servant."

"Since you're a soldier," Charley said, "you
might as well get used to it."

Jack was on thin ice. Most of our party were

from the South and were a little touchy about the views of outsiders. Being from Philadelphia didn't mean so much to us as it meant to Jack.

"Captain Clark owns slaves," I said. That was true. In fact, he had a huge black man named York along as his personal servant. "Captain Clark doesn't seem to bother you."

"Maybe you've just been living among slaves too long," Jack said.

"Maybe I have," I said. "And so I know more about them than you do in Philadelphia."

"You know about the wharf rats in Wheeling," Jack said, sneering.

"You boys got Captain Lewis all wrong," Charley said. "Captain Lewis don't know you exist."

"What do you mean, Charley?" I asked.

Charley Floyd's pale eyes narrowed slightly. He was the most deliberate man.

"Captain Lewis, he's got his mind set on grander things, grander things than even this here expedition. If he's thinking about you at all, which I doubt, he's thinking that you're one more hand to his purpose, nothing more."

I turned to him in surprise. "What 'grand things' are you talking about, Charley?"

Charley gave his familiar glance around, then said, "We're rowing Captain Lewis to glory."

"Well, I'm not," Jack said. "I'm not going to stand still for it."

"You can always desert," Charley said.

Jack smiled, a cold little twitch of a smile. "I won't desert," he said. "And I won't be spit on, neither."

Since Captain Lewis didn't tell us anything, our band was alive with rumors. Charley Floyd said that the plan was to winter at Fort Kaskaskia. Charley had heard it from Nat Pryor, and Nat seemed to know things nobody else knew. Nat was Charley Floyd's cousin. He was one of your lanky Kentuckians, all wrists and joints and Adam's apple, and silent as a cemetery.

"We only got twenty men so far," Charley confided. "Nat told me that's not half enough. Wait and see. We'll be sitting in Kaskasky when the river's froze."

When we finally got in sight of Fort Kaskaskia, the log huts with their smoking chimneys looked good to me. I began to hope that Charley and Nat were right and that we had reached our winter quarters. A cannon roared, and the commanding officer came down to welcome us.

For a moment I thought I had slipped my mooring. The captain at Fort Kaskaskia was the spit and image of Daniel Bissell back at Fort Massac. I guessed that the month of chilblains, frostbite, blisters, and Jack Newman had finally done for me.

But the mystery was soon solved. This one was *Russell* Bissell, brother to Daniel. Both of them were captains and Regular Army from Connecticut.

The Frenchmen had already pulled their pirogue up onto the mudflats and waded ashore. Jack Newman was talking with Captain Bissell. We could see him laughing and preening himself and waving his arms in the direction of our keelboat as if he were our commander himself.

Captain Lewis had put on his blue uniform coat in honor of the occasion. He jumped up on the roof of the forecastle and began to shout out orders: "Steady . . . More starboard . . . starboard! Hold her . . . HOLD her!"

I didn't quite see the need, since Charley Floyd was at the steering oar. He had brought us through a month of snags and riffles, never failing to land us easy.

Captain Lewis was in a sweat to get off, and I thought there was even more saluting and pomp than there had ever been when we left Fort Massac. He swept by Jack as if he were a stump.

A couple of minutes of saluting and jabbering went by before he remembered to introduce Captain Clark.

Captain Bissell brightened up and said he was honored to meet him and had known his older brother General George Rogers Clark and what a fine patriot he was and the bravest of the brave.

Captain Clark stood there smiling and saying nothing and taking it all in until Captain Lewis changed the subject.

"You're mighty welcome here," Captain Bissell said. "We know your orders are direct from President Jefferson, and such as we have here is at your service."

He was like his brother and like a lot of officers in those early days — manly, direct, and honest soldiers who asked nothing and feared nobody.

Charley and I were helping to unload the boats, and we could hear them talking plainly. Captain Lewis was going on about his troubles with the boat-builder back at Pittsburgh and how he had fallen several months behind. He worked in President Jefferson pretty regularly and allowed as how the purchase of the whole of the Louisiana Territory from Napoleon made it even more important to get on up the Missouri. But he was stalled. He still needed men, and winter was closing in.

"I've decided," he said to Captain Bissell, "to winter at the mouth of the Missouri. We'll build a camp on the east shore across from Saint Louis and then be ready to start with the spring thaw. It will give me a chance to make soldiers out of some of these . . ."

Captain Lewis stopped short and swung his arm in a circle toward us.

That first meeting between Captain Bissell and

our captains was all flapdoodle, but by the time we left Fort Kaskaskia you'd have needed a case knife to scrape off the frost. The night before we left, we heard that the two best men in Kaskaskia, John Ordway and Patrick Gass, were going to come along.

I don't know who talked to them, Captain Lewis or Captain Clark, but my guess is that it was William Clark. When he told you what you could expect to get out of it for yourself, the ready cash and the free land, you knew that it tasted like sand or swamp water on his tongue. It was when he described the wilderness, green and empty and stretching out to God knows where, that you couldn't wait to set out at sunrise.

The news of his loss hit Captain Bissell between wind and water. He offered Ordway and Gass sure promotions and the advantages of garrison life. In that he showed poor judgment. Ordway was already a sergeant and hadn't become a soldier to lead a peaceful life. To prove it he had a jagged purple scar in one shoulder where the arrow of an Iroquois had gone in and come out. He was a New Hampshireman and, what was more, a God-fearing man. As plain as one of the old Puritans, Sergeant Ordway concluded that exploring was his duty and that Captain Bissell was the voice of the Devil.

Pat Gass had been a sergeant several times, but it never lasted. He had such a powerful thirst. One look at the angle of Pat's jaw and you might as well give over. Pat had set his mind. A natural-born rover was Pat Gass.

Captain Bissell swallowed his loss sufficiently to invite our captains up to dinner the last evening at Fort Kaskaskia. George Drewyer's gun had been active and we had a feast ourselves. We were lolling around the campfire, half-asleep, when we heard something off in the forest.

Charley Floyd said, "What was that?"

I said it was an owl, but Charley said if it was an owl he sure hadn't got the news about temperance.

Then we heard a "whoo-oop!" and a "yip!" or two. These shouts were followed by a great thrashing and crashing. Out of the woods came our new comrade, Patrick Gass, with a gallon jug swinging at the end of his right arm like a pendulum. When he saw the fire, he came over, listing hard to starboard, and demanded to know who we were.

He listened very gravely as Charley Floyd pronounced our names all round. He nodded to each in turn and bowed so low that he was in constant danger of standing on his ear.

"Whoo-oop!" he shouted. "Pass the jug!"

It made its way around the circle and we each had a swig. It was corn whiskey and bit like a copperhead.

"Round again!" Pat hollered, and we all did as ordered.

Several of the Frenchmen, looking mighty thirsty, appeared out of the shadows. Pat greeted them with grunts and squawks, which we all took for French, not knowing better, and under the circumstances the Frenchmen weren't too particular. They seized the jug and took uncommonly long pulls.

"Easy! Easy!" Pat cautioned, falling back on English in this crisis.

He retrieved the jug, took a long drink, and broke into song:

> "Never no bairn and never no wife.
> The jolly raftsman's is the only life.
> Too-roo, too-roo, too-ree-ay."

The boys commenced to hoot and holler to drown him out, and old Pat took fire.

"Beware, gentlemen, beware!" he cried, pulling off his buckskin coat and throwing it on the ground. "I'm Patrick Gass. Fangs like a rattler, claws like a grizzly, horns like a mad bad bull! Beware, gentlemen, beware!"

Nat Pryor began to clap his hands and the others took it up. One of the Frenchmen produced a jew's-harp and Pat began to dance a jig. It was a sight to see. A cow could have danced more graceful than did Pat Gass. He took on so, he could have made a sheep smile.

"Whoo-oop!" Pat shouted through the din. "Yip!

Raw flesh for supper washed down with buffalo blood! Them's my victuals."

At that everybody cheered and Pat kicked up his heels. He came down and stood still, grinning at us. His eyes went glazed. Without warning, he went all loose and tottery like a rag doll sprung at every joint, and sank down in a heap by the fire.

Nat Pryor walked over to him and nudged him with the toe of his boot.

"Too much buffalo blood," Nat observed. He picked up the jug and gave it a shake. "Precious little left," he said. "More's the pity." He held it up to the fire. "We may as well finish it off."

"Why not?" Charley said. "He cain't carry it all the way to the Pacific."

I slept badly, with that corn whiskey on my stomach, and dreamed of earthquakes.

In the dawn somebody was singing. The morning was gray and damp and my eyelashes were sticky with frost. I rubbed the sleep from my eyes and propped myself up on one elbow. Down by the river, singing at the top of his lungs, was Pat Gass. He had plunged into the icy Mississippi and was now standing naked before a roaring fire and shaking himself dry like an old bulldog.

I crawled out of my blankets and hurried over to the fire to get warm. The Frenchmen were stirring but no one else.

"You're up early, laddie," Pat said. He looked as fresh as if he had drunk warm milk and slept in a feather tester. "What's your name?"

I guess he had forgotten our introduction of the night before.

"Hugh McNeal," I said.

"Well, Hugh McNeal, you're not long gone from your mother's apron."

Pat had small gray eyes set close together. Later, when we elected him sergeant, he would storm at us till his brow was black, but his eyes always belied him. Everything they clapped on amused him.

"Where ye from?" he demanded.

"I joined the party at Fort Massac."

"No wonder ye joined. That's a dreary corner of the world."

"I know it."

"How long have ye been in this Army?"

"About six months."

"You're young and green for this adventure. I wonder that the captains would enlist ye."

"So do I."

"Are ye not afeard?"

"Afraid of what?"

"Why, of the Indians. Of these high and mighty captains leading us out there and getting us lost? Or ill and dying in some prairie far from home and mother?" Pat was bent over, pulling on his leather breeches, and I couldn't see his face.

"At least it's better than chopping wood in a fort," I said.

Pat was struggling to pull his shirt over his heavy chest and shoulders. He finally came up out of his collar, puffing like a man surfacing for air.

"There's a lot of land out there," he said, and waved his arm westward. "The savages have ways of showing us we ain't wanted."

"So I've heard."

"You've heard, have you? Well, I've *seen*."

Pat was combing his beard with his fingers.

"It's not so bad if you're a woman," he said. "It's fast. They drive stakes through your body and into the ground. Swift and sure."

"What about men?"

"I remember once, I was about your age. We were scattered by an ambush and ran for dear life. When we went back to gather up our dead, come to find out the mouths of the corpses were stuffed with dirt. You see, them savages had ways of learning us. If we wanted their land, we could eat it."

"I've heard that they do that."

"But you ain't seen it. I *seen* it. I mean a field filled with the dead laying all about, each one scalped as neat as the root of a carrot. Ghastly it was. The morning was chill, like today, and from each warm and bloody head a little puff of mist was rising. You ever seen a cornfield filled with pumpkins?"

I nodded.

"That's what they looked like — pumpkins scattered about a cornfield."

Pat leaned toward me and his beady eyes twinkled.

"Who knows," he said, "what we'll see before we see the end of this here journey?"

6

Winter Quarters

Our captains chose a site for our winter camp on the east bank of the Mississippi at Wood River, just across from the mouth of the Missouri. It's easy to forget how slow news traveled in those days. Nobody in the Upper Mississippi knew that President Jefferson had bought all of Louisiana from Napoleon. So we camped on the American side and bided our time until we could lay claim to it all.

All winter long we looked across at the muddy Missouri spilling into the Mississippi. By late winter great chunks of filthy ice were piled up in its mouth. "Like rotten teeth to chew us raw," Pat Gass said.

The winter dragged on. Nobody knew quite how it happened, or that it was happening at all, but during the first months of 1804 a score of ornery, cantankerous soldiers set about wintering at Wood River Camp and by spring that same riffraff had been turned into a seasoned, disciplined Corps of Discovery.

They were as sturdy a crowd of men as ever I met before or since, indifferent to hardship and asking nothing more than to be left alone. Nothing short of gunpowder and shot could have molded them into a force except a great purpose and a great leader. The credit goes to Captain William Clark. Captain Lewis could have done it too. You could not fault him as a soldier, and he would brook no foolishness in training troops. But he was always off gallivanting, either to St. Louis to meddle in politics or downriver at the village of Cahokia to scrounge for supplies.

Captain Lewis would show up when least expected, striding about the camp in his blue uniform and finding fault. The blacksmiths, he allowed, were too slow, nothing like as fast as the ones he remembered back in Virginia. The men he set to making sugar had got it all wrong. He wasn't bashful about making his views known on all subjects. Captain Clark would follow him around the camp on their tours of inspection, nodding his head once in a while but mostly keeping mum.

"They ain't pullin' like a team," Charley Floyd said. "Lewis he got his ears laid back and afore long he's gonna kick."

Charley was right. Captain Lewis finally let fly, and the dust cloud was considerable. It was George Drewyer set him off.

Our captains didn't see eye to eye on George Drewyer. Captain Lewis thought him a little too neglectful of what was due an Army officer. Unlike the rest of us, George Drewyer was not enlisted in the Army but was paid to be our scout and interpreter. When Captain Lewis was giving him orders, George had a way of rummaging through his pockets in search of a twist of tobacco or pulling out his hunting knife to pare his fingernails. He would gape or scratch his belly or clean out his ears with his little finger.

All that didn't bother Captain Clark. He knew a good man when he saw one. If in the strain of raising a roof or launching a pirogue, somebody forgot and called him "Billy" to his face, Captain Clark let it pass. He knew to a hair's-breadth when to rebuke and when to ignore. So he tolerated George Drewyer's odd ways. They weren't intended to be personal, and there was no point in taking them so.

Well, we got up one morning to find that Captain Lewis had come back during the night. Something was eating him, for his mouth was tight as a seam. After breakfast he and Captain Clark set out for a round of inspection of Wood River Camp.

We had made good progress. The sawyers, lashed by the tongue of Pat Gass, had finished our huts. We were living warm and dry. Captain Clark had put me to work on the keelboat. That would have been fine with me, except that he told Jack Newman to help me all he could. Enough that Jack was all thumbs and much of what he did I had to undo. But he also grumbled all day long, as irksome as a yelping cur tied to a stake.

A better worker was Moses Reed, who had joined us at Kaskaskia. Unlike Jack, he'd rather see the job done right than wrong, but he could match Jack in grousing. He was tall, the tallest in our party, with round, sloping shoulders and long, powerful arms. He was guarded, was Moses Reed, and for all his talk we never knew quite what to make of him.

Moses and I had fitted new hinges to the lids of the lockers in the keelboat so that in case of Indian attack they could be thrown up to form a kind of breastwork for defense. We'd done the best we could, given the job we had inherited from that dunderhead back at Pittsburgh. The oarlocks in the bow had been so badly designed that we ripped them all out and reset them.

Finally, we mounted the brass cannon on the stern so that it would sweep the shore and discourage any attack on our rear. I had talked over the changes with Captain Clark, and he had told me to go ahead. I judged even my pa, who was particular, would have approved.

From down at the river we could see the two captains walking about the camp. After a while I saw them coming toward the keelboat. I got myself occupied with a balky hinge.

Captain Lewis came on board and stood for a moment looking at the cannon. He knelt down, swung it back and forth, and then got up. I was watching out of the tail of my eye. If he was satisfied, he didn't show it.

He walked up the boat and, one by one, lifted the lids of the lockers and slammed them down. The whole boat shook each time; if one of those hinges had been loose, it would have sprung. If they didn't close to please him, he threw them back with a crash and left them open.

When he reached us, he said, "Those I left open can be improved. Fix them."

"The lids are warped," I said, none too respectfully I'm afraid, for to tell the truth I had worked hard on those lids and each one was much better than I had found it.

"If you can't fix them," he said sharply, "perhaps there's somebody can."

"The wood was green," I said. "If it warped, you can't flatten it out now." I added a "sir," but a trifle tardy.

"I know that." Captain Lewis gave me a sour look. After a moment his eye caught the changes in the oarlocks. His lips got tighter and he turned to me.

"*You* did that, did you?"

"Yes . . . Captain."

"And *you* thought those changes ought to be made?"

"I did."

"You're a judge of such things, are you?"

I saw we were approaching rapids, too late to backwater.

"Whoever made those oarlocks," I said, "was drunk or crazy."

The corner of Captain Lewis's mouth began to twitch as though it had a life of its own.

He turned to Jack and Moses and said, "Did you work on this?"

They both nodded but said nothing. I guess they figured that since I had appointed myself their leader, now I could lead.

Then Captain Lewis let rip. I never saw an officer so angry. He began by laying me out for fiddling with the design of "his" keelboat. He had planned it, and planned it well, and he wouldn't have it ruined by some upstart son of a riverman.

I started to protest at that, but he shouted me down. I'd have had more chance of throwing myself in front of a landslide. When he had done with me, Captain Lewis started on Jack and Moses. They had backed off some from the heat, but he stomped after them, shouting all the while. Somehow he had got them confused in his mind with the men George Drewyer had enlisted in Tennessee.

"You two!" he cried. "You think you can act like Drewyer, do what you bloody please!" He stamped his foot on the deck. "I won't have it!" he shouted.

Both Jack and Moses were tall. Captain Lewis stood before them, his face, scarlet with anger, thrust up into theirs.

They were too startled to try to defend themselves. They stood there with their eyes bugging, leaning backward so as not to get scorched.

Finally, Captain Lewis stopped, or rather he seemed to run down. He stood there, red-faced and panting.

"Captain Lewis."

The voice was Captain Clark's. It sounded quiet but mighty clear, like a voice coming across a valley.

Captain Lewis swung around. I think that he had completely forgotten that Captain Clark was there. I'm sure I'd forgotten him.

"Captain Lewis," Captain Clark said, "these are not George Drewyer's men. These men were enlisted by me, as perhaps you will recall, at Fort Massac and Fort Kaskaskia. And what they have done on this boat, they have done by my orders."

Captain Clark's voice was low, but it was steady and it was cold as ice.

Captain Lewis looked back and forth between us, and for just a moment I thought he was going to let rip again. But suddenly he seemed to recollect himself. He passed his hand over his brow and rubbed his eyes.

"Of course," he mumbled. "Of course."

Captain Lewis turned and made his way to the stern, Captain Clark following in his wake.

After that, things changed. Until then we all considered that we were under the command of the great Meriwether Lewis, gentleman from Virginia and kinsman of President Jefferson. But after that morning on the keelboat, we all understood what had not been exactly clear before. We were under the command of Lewis *and* Clark.

❧ 7 ❧

A Midnight Dip in the Mississippi

The winter dragged on at Wood River Camp. By March everything was ready, and there was nothing left to do but wait for the spring thaw. At night we could hear the grinding and crashing as the blocks of ice broke up in the river mouth. The brown water came roiling into the Mississippi, and we could see the dark tangles of tree roots tumbling over and over with the current. Every once in a while a log would leap out of a wave like a battering ram. But as fearsome as the Missouri looked, we were ready for it.

Captain Clark began to have trouble keeping us busy. Every day we had target practice, although there wasn't a man along who hadn't been a crack shot as long as he could remember. To liven it up Captain Clark offered a dipper of whiskey as a prize to the best marksman. When he heard that, George Drewyer took an interest in the proceedings. That was the end of the sport.

George was the coolest marksman I ever saw. He

would loll against a tree or stretch out on the ground, letting everyone else go first. When all had fired, he would shamble up to the line, throw his rifle to his shoulder as if he had nothing more serious in mind than firing a salute in the air. Suddenly his body would go still as a statue, the trigger would click, the powder flash, and the lead sink into the heart of the target. Several men would rush to see, but George always turned away with a little gesture of contempt.

Once Pat Gass, already awash with more than a dipper of whiskey and feeling ornery because he wasn't going to win some more, let out one of his yips in George's ear just as he squeezed off his shot. George might have been deaf as a post for all it bothered him. He never flickered, and as neatly as you please drove in the lead and drained off the whiskey without even so much as a nod in the direction of old Pat.

Pat stood swaying in the sunlight, flushed and breathing hard, looking mighty foolish.

Pat was often drunk that winter, as were several of the other veterans who had, even in that deserted edge of the world, sniffed out a shed where for a few coppers you could get a cup of corn whiskey. The bottomlands about the mouth of the Missouri were rich farming country. Squatters had moved in here and there, and they were glad to trade whiskey for the ready cash that soldiers always had and were always ready to spend.

In March Captain Lewis sent word from St. Louis to tell Captain Clark to come over for some political meeting connected with the transfer of Louisiana to the United States. Captain Clark hurried off on horseback, leaving Sergeant Ordway acting as commander while he was gone. Hardly had the hoofbeats died away when Jack Newman and Moses Reed appeared at the keelboat, where I was making extra oars out of ash saplings.

"We think we can get some whiskey for tonight," Moses said. "Do you want a share?"

"You mean from the company stores?"

The whiskey for the men was kept under lock and key. John Ordway was in charge of it, and he was not the man to let it out to the likes of Jack and Moses.

"Reuben Field knows a farmer as will sell," Moses said. Reuben was older than we were, had fought Indians in Kentucky, and except for George Drewyer was the best hunter in the party. And only Pat Gass had a better nose for whiskey.

"How much?" I asked.

"A dollar if you want in."

"A dollar!"

"That's it. A dollar."

"But a dollar's a week's wages."

"So it is," Moses said. "You in or out?"

"What about Ordway?"

"What about him?" Jack said.

"Will he let you?"

"We ain't asking him," Moses said. "Not that he'll ever know."

"And if he knows," Jack added, "what will he do?"

"He can report it to the captains," I said.

"He can," Jack said, "but he won't. He likes being sergeant so much, he ain't likely to riffle the waters about a jug."

"Don't count on it," I said.

"Those captains are livin' high on the hog," Moses said. "You think they ain't drinkin' with the quality over there in Saint Louis? So high and mighty, they are. Blast their eyes anyhow! Well, what are you goin' to do? Git in or git out!"

"I'm out," I said.

They went off, their heads together, mumbling.

The afternoon stretched out slow and uneasy. Sergeant Ordway walked about the camp talking to the knots of men who were letting on to work. But with the captains both away, you could feel the company sag. The March day was sticky and overcast, a day to give you the fantods. The sky was black in the east and you could hear thunder rumbling around the edges.

In the middle of the afternoon Jack and Moses and Reuben Field came back into camp. They had been sent out on a hunting party. Instead of reporting to Sergeant Ordway, they came down to the river, where I was just finishing up.

"You're a good worker, Hugh," Moses shouted. "You must be working up a sweat."

I called back something, I forget what, and Moses said, "Keep at it, Private. You'll be a corporal yet."

They all laughed at that, fit to kill.

Sergeant Ordway heard them and came ambling down to the river. He was looking jumpy, and you could tell that being in charge of that crew was getting to him.

"Why didn't you report when you got back?" he demanded.

Reuben Field got to his feet. He swayed a little. "Nothing to report," he said, none too pleasantly. His narrow, leathery face was uncommonly red.

"You mean you came back empty-handed?"

Reuben smiled. "That's about the size of it," he said. "Empty-handed."

Sergeant Ordway was a big, slow-moving man, generally calm as a pond at low water. But he was heating up. He turned on Jack and Moses.

"Get up!" he ordered.

They straggled to their feet, taking their time about it.

"The three of you get going," Sergeant Ordway said. "And don't come back until you get something."

That was a mistake. A hunter can't help it if there's no game, and the weather was against them.

Reuben saw he had an edge. He looked Sergeant Ordway up and down, studying him as if he weren't quite bright, then slowly shook his head from side to side. Jack and Moses stood behind him, giggling and nudging one another.

"You're not going?" Sergeant Ordway said.

Reuben Field shook his head again. "I'm not a-going hunting," he said. "I'm no blamed fool."

"You're not going?" Ordway said again, this time very slow and clear.

"No!"

Ordway turned to me. "Did you hear that, McNeal?"

The three swung around and stared at me. "Did you hear it?" he repeated.

I nodded.

"Remember it," Sergeant Ordway said.

He turned and walked off toward the huts.

When he was out of earshot, Reuben Field gave me a threatening look. "If you're quick," he said, "you'll forget it."

They fell to muttering among themselves, and I went back to work. After a while they drifted off up the hill.

Supper that night was a glum affair. Since the hunting party had not brought in any game, we ate what jerked venison there was about the camp and some sourdough bread and a few berries. The bad food put everybody out of sorts. Sergeant Ordway unlocked the stores and poured out the usual allowance of whiskey, letting the dipper slosh over a bit as if he knew that the troops were feeling mutinous.

Somewhere in the trees beyond our clearing, the boys had stored their jug. As soon as it was dark, men began to drift away from the fire and after an interval come back, looking flushed and jovial.

Charley Floyd came over and flopped down beside me.

"You get some?" he asked.

"I don't want any," I said.

"What?" He couldn't believe his ears. "Come on," he said. "I'll show you where it is."

I shook my head.

"Come on," he insisted.

"I didn't put in a dollar."

Charley gave me a puzzled look. He didn't say anything more, and the next time I looked around he was gone.

Peter Cruzatte, an enlistee from St. Louis whose mother was an Omaha Indian, got out his fiddle and began to play. At once Pat Gass broke out in a dance.

"I'm most savagerous!" he shouted. "Looky!"

Somebody threw a pile of brush onto the fire, and the clearing burst into light.

Nat Pryor grabbed Pat and they began a Virginia reel, bowing and curtsying and swinging one another around in the most comical manner. Before long a dozen or more of the men were doing a jig.

I judged I had made a mistake, not putting in

my dollar. When the fire burned down a bit, I drifted off into the shadows and into my hut. I crawled under my robe and lay in the darkness, listening to the shouting and the wild screeching of Peter Cruzatte's fiddle. I dozed for a long time and finally fell off to sleep.

Suddenly I was wide awake. I could hear feet pounding and voices shouting. I opened my eyes. The hut was pitch black. Then very clearly I could hear shouts of "The witness! He's in thar! Git him! The witness!"

Somebody thrust a torch into the hut. At first I was blinded by the flame, and then I made out the raw, pinched face of Reuben Field, slick and greasy in the firelight.

"Thar he is!" Reuben shouted. "Git him."

Rough hands grabbed me. I tried to squirm free, but I was tangled in my robe.

"Greased pig!" somebody panted.

A heavy fist caught me on the ear, and a knuckle gouged into my cheek. I tried to strike back. I caught somebody, for I heard a grunt, but it was a glancing blow, not a solid hit. I sank my teeth into somebody's arm and tasted blood. Whoever I got let out a yell and hit me a good one in the side of my head with his fist. Then my arms were pinned to my sides.

I felt myself hoisted aloft by a dozen hands and I knew I was being carried to the river. I caught a glimpse of the fire, now burned almost to ashes, and men sprawled about it, drunk or asleep.

I picked out the voices of Jack Newman and Moses Reed, shouting, "Let him fly!"

The next thing, I felt the icy shock as the black water of the Mississippi River closed over my head.

I stayed underwater until my lungs were empty, and let the current carry me downstream.

When I came to the surface, I took a quick breath and went under again. When I bobbed up once more, I was well downstream. Back on shore I could see Reuben Field holding the torch out over the water and faces peering about and men shouting, "Whar'd he go? McNeal! McNeal!"

I let myself drift along until I couldn't stand the cold any longer. I caught hold of a bough hanging out over the river. The bank was slimy and the muck squished up between my toes. I crawled out on my knees and lay there, panting in the mud, until my breath came back.

The air felt warmer than the water, and I pulled off my shirt and wrung it out. I sat down naked between the roots of a tree and put my head back against the trunk. I was breathing hard and shaking like a willow in a storm. I rubbed my arms and legs hard and tried to heat up. The night was black as a coal cellar, with only the Mississippi murmuring in the darkness.

Then I heard a noise. And then another. I was

scared. You could hear the wolves howling at night, and I didn't know what else might be prowling around in the blackness. I stopped breathing and lay against the tree as still as a possum. Then I knew. The sound was footsteps. No wolf would have let on he was coming.

I heard the branches rustling and twigs snapping underfoot. Then everything went still as death and somebody was standing not ten feet away from me. I wondered whether it was Reuben Field, not content just to dunk me but ready to drown me as well.

"Who's there?" I blurted out. My voice was shaking so, I could hardly speak.

"Hugh?"

"Who is it?"

I knew the voice but I couldn't place it in the blackness.

"Charley."

When I heard who it was, I could have cried with relief.

"Where are you?" Charley asked. "It's blacker than the inside of a cow."

"Over here."

Charley edged over and hunkered down.

"I brung this."

He tossed me a buffalo robe. I pulled it round me, but I couldn't stop shivering.

"Odd time for swimming," Charley observed. Coming out of the pitch darkness, his voice sounded strange, deeper than when you could see his pale eyes.

"I needed a wash," I said, as best I could. I could hardly talk, my teeth were chattering so.

I must have sounded pretty bad, for Charley said, "You all right?"

"I sure took on a cargo of Mississippi mud," I said.

"Don't take it personal," Charley said. "The boys are just having some fun."

"Don't worry," I said. "It's a long journey. There'll be lots of time to even things up."

Although I could see only a shape beside me, I knew Charley was looking around before he spoke.

"Seems like it would be easier to pay the dollar," he said.

"Why should I pay for the likes of them?"

"Why not treat 'em?" Charley said.

Charley was just too dim to get the point. The talk was going nowhere.

"Let's go," I said.

We made our way slowly back to camp, tripping over tree roots and snagging ourselves in vines and underbrush. I got on board the keelboat and let myself down into the forecastle. The captains would never know I'd been there. I wasn't too keen on going back to my hut and running into Reuben Field twice in one night.

"You sure you're all right?" Charley said.

"I'm all right."

In the morning the camp was about as gay as a funeral. Sergeant Ordway, acting as if nothing had happened, set the men to cleaning up. My ear was puffed up like a cabbage. I reckoned I had given Jack Newman equal measure, for his left eye was shut tight as a clam. Moses Reed had an angry scratch across his cheek.

Our captains rode into camp about the middle of the afternoon. They went at once to their hut, and Sergeant Ordway was in there with them a long time. When he finally came out, we all knew that something was up. He passed the word that there would be a parade at sunset.

That evening we lined up on parade. Both Captain Lewis and Captain Clark had put on their officer's uniforms. Captain Lewis called out Sergeant Ordway. He had his orders written out and he read them to us. John was not much of a reader and he stumbled some, but we all got the point.

I thought there would be some lashes laid on, but the captains were content with a warning. Reuben Field was singled out by name as somebody more was expected from, and he squirmed. When John Ordway was finished, we knew the next time there would be lashes for the offenders. As it turned out, the next time was only a few weeks away.

What Charley said about paying the dollar bothered me no end. That stuck in my craw. Although I hated to admit it, Charley had a point. It seemed folly to be on bad terms with people you live with every day. I decided the next time I would pay the dollar.

But after I decided, I still couldn't be sure. Was it because, as Charley said, it was the sensible thing to do? Or, as I fingered my swollen ear, was I scared of what would happen if I didn't pay up?

Next time, I figured I wouldn't puzzle my head. I'd just pay the dollar and be done with it.

❧ 8 ❧
The Party Starts Out

Over the winter the Corps of Discovery had grown to forty-seven men. The main party consisted of our two captains and twenty-nine soldiers enlisted for the journey. Ten Frenchmen — we called them *engagés* — had been hired to tote supplies and help ward off Indian attacks. They rowed the red pirogue, which was mounted with a big old blunderbuss. Those Frenchmen would laugh and stroke the barrel of that blunderbuss as if it were the neck of a favorite pony. Finally, an escort of six soldiers in the white pirogue would go as far as our winter quarters and then turn back.

We were into the middle of May before we finally shoved off. The ice was gone from the Missouri but it was as brown as a new-plowed field. Captain Lewis, as usual, was off somewhere and would join us up the river. So the order to move out came from Captain Clark. The Sunday we were to leave dawned dark and rainy, a soggy, drenching downpour. Even our buckskins were soaked by the time the keelboat and the two pirogue were loaded. Wet buckskin today meant buckskin stiff as birch bark tomorrow.

The sun, looking a little dim and uncertain, finally poked through the overcast. The breeze freshened out of the southeast as the rain slackened, a forwarding wind and a good omen. Overhead the sky was cornflower blue, and on the edges clouds piled up like haystacks.

Captain Clark was in high good humor, laughing and leaping about like a boy. His red hair was plastered down over his forehead, and his face shone with the rain. When all was ready, he stood in the bow of the keelboat, brandished his sword in the air for the benefit of a few squatters standing on the shore, and shouted out, "Sail!"

We answered with a cheer, and the stragglers on the shore echoed our shouts.

Our two captains divided the privates up into three squads of about nine each under Sergeants John Ordway, Nat Pryor, and Charley Floyd. To my great relief I was named to Charley's squad, although Reuben Field and Jack Newman were also in it. What with one thing and another, they gave me no rest.

"We drew the sailor boy," Reuben said with a sneer. His slick, narrow face pitted with smallpox scars looked meaner than ever.

Jack snickered but didn't say anything.

"Should we trust the sails to you galoots?" Pat

Gass said to them. Reuben and Jack fell silent. They didn't want to tangle with old Pat. As soon take on a grizzly as Pat Gass.

We fell to, twenty-two men at the oars. We pulled and grunted against that wild current. A broken oar, a sudden cross-current, a snag, then wild shouts and confusion as we slipped back, the keelboat spinning out of control, each lost moment costing us the sweat of a half-hour.

"Hold! Hold, ye varmints!" Pat Gass would shout.

Charley Floyd would slam down the helm, trying to keep her bow in the current.

The keelboat lurched and the decks trembled beneath our oars. The hull plunged and rolled, pitching the rowers against one another.

Amidst the roar Pat's voice sang out, "Pull! Pull, lads! Heave!"

From the red pirogue the Frenchmen would rest on their oars and laugh at our plight, shouting at us in their crazy tongue.

Just being on the move put us all in better spirits. Our bare backs turned bronze in the June sunlight, and we gorged on wild plums, raspberries, and apples. We pulled catfish from the river as fast as we could eat them. Deer were everywhere, their signs as plentiful as hog tracks on a farm. At night we didn't bother to pitch our tents. We'd lie on the banks looking up at the stars and watching the Great Bear swing around the North Star.

Most nights I slept the sleep of the dead. But some nights I'd come wide awake at a shriek in the forest and toss in my blankets till sunrise, remembering the scalp that George Drewyer had tucked beneath his shirt.

So far even George Drewyer hadn't seen any Indians to speak of, although nobody needed to be told to keep a sharp lookout. Nat Pryor was in charge of defense. When we got to shore at night, it was his job to post the sentinels and pick out the campsite. Six men would fan out through the brush or the forest for a hundred yards or more, keeping low to the ground and gliding swiftly from tree to tree, seeking cover. Day after day we saw nothing but an occasional trapper rafting downstream with his load of beaver skins. None of us could throw off the feeling that, behind those thickets and vines, savage eyes were following each step deeper into the forest.

Jack Newman still fumed at Captain Lewis for the times he made him row in the pirogue. In that he had a point, I think, for Jack was the only soldier of the permanent party who got that duty. If he had wanted to, Captain Lewis could have spread the job around. But he didn't want to. Jack nettled Captain Lewis. You could tell. One incident, in particular, sticks in my memory.

We had stopped at midday to eat and to rest from the blazing July heat. Our two captains were at work with a sextant, trying to find out where we were in that wilderness. While the rest of us dozed in such shade as we could find, they sat on a log puzzling over their figures. Although they kept chuckling over their error to each other, we could hear a little strain in their voices. We were either lost or close to it.

Jack must have been listening, for he got up and went over to them.

"May I have a look, sir?" he asked.

Captain Lewis didn't even look up.

Captain Clark handed him the paper. "More power to you, Jack," he said. "Have a gander."

Jack studied the page for a minute, then pointed with his finger. "That's it," he said. "There's the problem. It's twelve degrees latitude."

Captain Clark studied it, his lips slowly forming the numbers as he went over the page.

"Blamed if he's not right," he said at last and slapped his thigh. "Where'd you learn navigation, Jack?"

"At the college at Philadelphia," Jack said.

Captain Clark handed the page to Captain Lewis. Well, Captain Lewis studied that page as if it were Holy Scripture. Finally, he looked up and nodded. That was all. He just nodded. Captain Clark said something else, but I didn't hear it. I was thinking that Captain Lewis didn't want to go to school to Jack Newman.

Jack might have got on better with Captain Lewis if it hadn't been for Moses Reed. Moses kept after Jack like a mosquito buzzing and pestering in the dark. Jack couldn't be set to jerking meat or pitching the tents but Moses found in it some plot of Captain Lewis.

"What are we doing out here?" Jack would ask.

"We're all crazy, that's what," Moses would answer. "And Lewis is the craziest of us all."

I was getting mighty tired of their complaints.

"Well, we're here," I said. "It's a little late in the day to change our minds."

"Who says we can't?' Jack said.

"What do you mean?"

"I mean, what's to keep us from cutting back?"

"That's desertion," I said.

"You catch on quick, McNeal, for a river rat," Moses said.

"What kind of a rat deserts?" I said.

"You're a born slave, McNeal," Jack said. "Keep it up. Lewis may buy you for his plantation when we get back."

Pat Gass had ambled up.

"I'm glad you fellows are so fierce," he said. "We'll need you for the Sioux."

Nobody said anything to that.

"You know the sign for the Sioux?" Pat asked.

We shook our heads.

Pat stuck out his forefinger like a knife blade and drew it slowly across his throat. His tongue lolled out and his eyeballs rolled up in his head.

We all laughed. But not too heartily.

"We run the risk," Jack said. "But if ever we get back from this crazy trip, the captains'll get the fame. What'll we get?" He curled his lip in a sneer. "A homestead."

"Why don't ye hurry back to yours?" Pat Gass said to him. "Mama's waiting at the door."

Jack didn't laugh but simply stared into the campfire.

We made our first long rest at the point where the River Platte joins the Missouri. We had been out over two months, and it was getting on toward August. Many of the men were suffering from boils, the cargo was mildewed and needed to be dried out, and the keelboat was battered from sandbars and snags.

After breakfast that first morning I was sitting on a cask by the river, repairing a moccasin thong, when Captain Lewis appeared. I hopped to attention, my moccasin in my hand. He told me to stand at ease.

The captain had come down to inspect the kegs of powder, barrels of flour and whiskey, and bales of trinkets for the Indian trade, all spread about to dry on a grassy slope. My knuckles were bloody from wrestling those casks out of the hold, through the narrow door of the cabin, and down a plank to shore. Captain Lewis started to walk among the supplies, poking about for trouble as usual, and

I followed along, feeling unsoldierly in one bare foot.

Suddenly he stopped and turned to me. "McNeal, starting today, you're in charge of transporting this cargo. I don't need to tell you how important that is. Get what help you need on my authority. I leave it to you."

"Yes, sir."

I thought, if I had offended him that morning at Fort Massac when I offered him some advice on how to trim a keelboat, he was getting his revenge. Loading cargo wasn't work for soldiers. It was slave labor, and Jack Newman would sneer when he heard about it. Still, it perked me up to be chosen, even for such a task.

Captain Lewis was in a good mood that morning, so I risked asking him a question about our supplies that had been bothering me since we left Wood River. We were carrying several hundred pounds of boxes labeled HARPERS FERRY ARSENAL. They were heaped in a pile, and when we reached them, I asked Captain Lewis what they were.

He smiled at the question. "That's the *Experiment*, McNeal."

"Sir?"

"The *Experiment*." He laughed aloud. "You don't like that keelboat. Very well, I see your point. Just be patient. When the Missouri gets too shallow for the keelboat, the *Experiment* will carry us."

Then he explained his plan. The blacksmiths at

Harpers Ferry had hammered out from his design an iron frame for a boat that could be carried in parts and put together when needed. The frame would be covered with elk and buffalo hides, Indian-fashion, the seams sealed with pitch, and we would all float down to the Pacific Ocean. Captain Lewis ran his hand over those boxes as he talked, warming to his plan. It sounded clever to me. I'd never have thought of it.

"When it's time to assemble it, I'm counting on you to be ready, McNeal. You're the boat-builder. Remember?"

And with a brisk order for me to get to work, he strode off.

I remember looking into Captain Lewis's face that morning. I noticed for the first time how that wilderness journey was leaving its mark on him. His nose and chin, so sharp you noticed them at once, seemed weathered to a finer edge by prairie winds and scorching heat. His hair had grown thick and wild, and it struck me that with his piercing eyes and that bronzed face he could look as savage as any Indian we were likely to meet on our journey.

His warning to be ready didn't bother me. I'd be ready.

The Missouri had swung from west to northwest. We were out in the middle of the prairie now, but with occasional bluffs rising up to provide good views up and down the river. Thick grass covered rich soil, and here and there the line of the horizon was broken with groves of walnut and oak.

But still the Indians didn't show. We were in the territory of the tribes of the Oto and Omaha. Both our captains thought it would be wise to stop until we could try to hold council with them and explain our mission.

Captain Clark named our stopping place Council Bluffs.

The second day in camp, Moses and Jack and I were sent out to bring in a deer that George Drewyer had shot. As soon as we were well out of sight and hearing, we sat down on a log to have a smoke. Moses was flushed and excited. You could tell something was up. He couldn't sit still but got up and paced back and forth.

"What's biting you?" Jack said.

Moses gave us one of his sly glances. He leaned forward and spoke in a whisper.

"I've decided," he said.

"You're crazy," Jack said.

I didn't know what they were talking about.

"Then you're not coming?" Moses said to Jack.

Jack shook his head. "Not me."

Moses turned to me. "You keep your mouth shut," he hissed.

"How are you going to do it?" Jack asked.

Moses looked around to be sure that nobody

could hear him, but we were screened from camp by the trees. "I'm going with one of the Frenchmen."

"Which one?"

"You'll find out soon enough."

"It's desertion," Jack said. "If they catch you, they'll shoot you."

"How will they catch me?"

"Lewis will catch you. He's as crazy as you are. He'll track you until he gets you."

"Lewis! He's got too much at stake to stop for me. He knows he's way behind where he wants to be. He'll consider himself well rid of me."

"He'll be right," I said.

Moses looked at me and I saw those big hands clench into fists. I began to regret my mouth, but Jack said, "You don't understand his kind of crazy. He'll hold up the whole party to run you to earth. You'll never make it, Moses."

"You!" Moses was looking at me. "Remember! Keep your mouth shut about this."

"You can do what you please for all of me," I said. "Good riddance."

"You won't change your mind?" Moses said to Jack.

"It's crazy," Jack said again. "You won't get away."

Suddenly we heard shouting from the camp and then gunfire, the signal to gather. We set off on the run. We could see Captain Clark racing about, his red hair blowing in the breeze. The camp was alive with men grabbing their rifles, forming up into ranks. And then we heard the shout that told all.

"Indians!"

❧ 9 ❧
Powwow

Both captains were rushing about the camp shouting orders. Only the Frenchmen showed no interest. They had been at work on the red pirogue. They put down their tools to watch us skittering about. One of them, who had been lying near the boat having a nap, raised up on his elbow, gazed sleepily about, then lay back down and pulled his hat over his eyes.

Six Oto chiefs were walking toward us across the prairie. Hanging back a hundred yards or so was a party of about twelve braves. We watched them come in their buffalo robes and feathers, and I felt my stomach cinch. They came on through the prairie grass, walking straight ahead, their faces as blank as owls. Then I saw that they had a white man in tow, a little, hairy, dried-up fellow with one eye and no teeth.

"Stand where you are," Captain Clark said to us quietly. "Have your rifles at the ready."

The two captains, empty-handed, started walking out toward the chiefs.

You had to hand it to them. They were as cool as Sunday and here come a passel of Baptists with nothing more in mind than to dip a sinner.

I stood watching those two small parties advance on each another through the prairie grass. The bowl of blue sky blazed with light, and the prairie stretched out to the brim. And here in the middle of the wilderness walked two American soldiers in deerskin and six Oto Indians in buffalo robes. We stood in silence and watched — three squads of soldiers hundreds of miles from home. The Indians seemed as natural out there as the elk and the deer. We were the strangers. Maybe, I thought, Jack Newman was right. What were we doing out there?

The captains turned and shouted for George Drewyer. The stringy little man with the chiefs was a Frenchman, so George would know what he was saying.

George ambled out, taking his good old time. After some talk, the whole party came into camp for a powwow. I couldn't get over those first Indians. I'd been listening to Pat Gass tell us about them, savages of gigantic size, fierce, treacherous and cruel, and hostile to white men. But these old chiefs looked as tame as goats and twice as mangy. They were smaller than any one of us, their skin slack on their necks like old women. They stood there, staring at us and scratching their lice. One thing was certain. If we were scared of them, they were just as scared of us.

Their head chief stood tense and silent in the middle of us, as though he might any moment charge or bolt. George Drewyer talked and then the stringy white man talked. There were long pauses while we all looked one another over. Then George and the Frenchman went at it again. Finally Captain Clark gave them pork and flour and meal, and they began to be easy. One of them hustled off, and later in the day a young brave came into camp with a pile of watermelons for us.

Next, Captain Lewis ordered John Ordway to take a mainsail and set it up on poles as a kind of awning. The Indians gathered in its shade and our men lined up on parade. What followed was comical enough, although none of us dared laugh. Out came Captain Lewis, all got up in his blue officer's uniform. First, he produced some medals he had brought along and gave one to each of the main chiefs.

Captain Lewis had also brought along some certificates and passed them out to some of the minor chiefs. Well, those chiefs didn't like getting a paper instead of a medal. They began to mutter and mumble among themselves. Suddenly an old chief got up and stumped over to Captain Lewis. He was a withered up old turkey with a great beak of a nose and a face as brown and cracked as a dry riverbed.

Old Turkey was so angry, he didn't know where to turn. He threw his certificate at the feet of Captain Lewis, trying at the same time to jump up and down on it. He lurched sideways and pitched over onto another chief, who caught him and helped him back up on his feet.

Then he grabbed at Captain Lewis and at George Drewyer and at the one-eyed Frenchman, turning from one to the other until we all thought he was going to fall down in a fit. But once he was in motion you could no more stop him than you could stop a thunderstorm. He kept pointing at the certificate, which was lying in the dirt, rather the worse for wear.

Pat Gass was grinning from ear to ear, and even that sober Puritan John Ordway was twinkling a little at the antics of the old Indian. Captain Lewis didn't quite see the joke. He let the certificate lie in the dirt, and his face was getting dark in a way that we had learned to respect.

Captain Clark saved the day. He fetched another medal, a large shiny one, made a little speech, of which Old Turkey understood not one word, and with much bowing presented it to him. Old Turkey snatched it from Captain Clark as though it were food and he hadn't eaten in a week. He hobbled back to his place under the sail and took his seat by the other chiefs. They grinned and showed their medals to one another like schoolgirls.

Then Captain Lewis reared back and made a

speech. You would have thought he was addressing the Congress. He sawed his arms in the air, bobbed his head about, and roared out one thing and another. The Indians sat with their black eyes fixed on his face, nodding their heads and fingering their medals.

I heard that speech so many times afterward that I could have given it myself by the end. The Great Chief of the Seventeen Great Nations of America had sent us to tell the Indians that they had a new White Father in Washington. The old fathers, the Spanish and the French, had crossed the great waters beyond the rising sun, never to return. Now the red children had to give up their French and Spanish medals and exchange them for American medals. From now on only American traders and vessels could pass.

The one-eyed Frenchman kept relaying all this to the Oto chiefs. The speech went on and on, and finally Captain Lewis lurched to a stop. Then he ordered the whiskey to be got out, and it was a good thing, because we were all dry. Things livened up considerably, but Captain Lewis had more big medicine. He had brought along a newfangled contraption called an air gun. He produced a bellows and pumped air into the gun. It shot pellets as fast as they could be dropped in, and it fired much faster than anyone could load, wad, and prime a Kentucky rifle. That air gun was almost as powerful as a rifle and it made only a pop and not a blast. With a Kentucky rifle, everyone within a country mile knew when it went off.

The Indians had been wary of their new white fathers, but now for the first time they dropped their grave looks. Awash with a gill of whiskey, they gathered about Captain Lewis, jabbering at him and snatching at the air gun.

That night they danced. It was a sight to see. They got themselves painted and greased and then they formed a circle around the fire. They commenced to whoop and holler to wake the dead. With the firelight glittering on their painted bodies and them twisting in all sorts of ways, you would have thought that the writhing of the tormented in Hell couldn't be worse. They beat on skins stretched over hoops and waved poles in the air decorated with what looked to me like the scalps of white men. It was enough to make you go cold all over to see them.

A warrior would suddenly leap up, raise his hands in the air to point to the different nations, and then make a speech. Without knowing a word, you could tell he was counting off the number of scalps he had taken, the number of horses he had stolen. They frisked about until the moon had set. Finally the whiskey wore off, and the dance came to an end.

It was agreed that we would camp with those

Indians. But I couldn't get off to sleep. I would close my eyes and begin to drift off. But just as I would fall into a drowse, I'd hear one of those braves let out a groan in his sleep, or a yelp, and I'd be wide awake with my hand on my throat, feeling from ear to ear and making sure it was still in one piece.

The second morning after we left Council Bluffs, Moses Reed was gone.

"He left his knife," Jack Newman said. "He went back to get it."

His eyes darted away from me when he said it, and I thought something was odd. Not that there was anything strange in going back for your knife. In the wilderness as soon lose your thumb as your knife. But still, something was peculiar in the way Jack said it.

Moses still wasn't back the next morning and neither was La Liberté, the Frenchman that Captain Clark sent to invite some more Oto chiefs to our camp.

Captain Clark came by our mess while I was cooking breakfast over the fire.

"We wonder if Reed got himself lost out on the prairie," Captain Clark said. "Do any of you know anything about it?"

Nobody answered. I was hunched down holding a skillet of frying fish over the fire.

"How about you, Newman?"

Jack shook his head.

"And you, McNeal?"

I felt Captain Clark's eyes on my back. I kept looking at the skillet and I shook my head.

Rumors flew about the camp all day that Moses Reed and La Liberté had fled. At dusk I saw Sergeant Ordway deep in talk with the two captains. At daybreak Captain Lewis sent George Drewyer and Reuben Field and two other men to find them and to bring them back. According to the story passed from man to man, Captain Lewis had told George Drewyer that if Moses did not give up peacefully, he was to be "put to death."

The search party was gone for ten days. Since we were threading our way through Indian country, more men were needed to stand guard, and that meant that fewer men were left to handle the keelboat and the pirogues. We'd been making about twenty miles a day up the Missouri, but now we dropped back to ten.

Captain Lewis was fuming at the delay, and we all gave him a wide berth. The middle of August had come and gone, and we were beginning to see the first signs of autumn. Our goal was the falls of the Missouri, and we were nowhere near them.

Captain Lewis would set off into the woods in the morning and return grim and silent.

Even Captain Clark, generally calm and good-natured, was showing the strain. Once Charley Floyd let the keelboat slide up on a sandbar. The rowers went over the side to pull it off, yelling and cursing Charley as they plunged into the water. The current churned up the brown mud, and the bottom sank under our feet. The men, up to their armpits in water, grabbed at the gunwales and struggled for a toehold in the muck. The clumsy boat settled so deep into the bar that we had to run a line to shore. With half the men in the water sputtering and cussing and the other half heaving the line on shore, the keelboat finally gave a lurch to starboard and slid off the bar.

Usually we would have cheered when the boat came off, but nobody was in the mood. Two men shouted that they had lost their moccasins in the thick sand. We spent a half-hour diving in the murk for them, and, at the end, Captain Clark tongue-lashed Charley Floyd. Charley stood silent, his flaxen hair plastered down over his scalp with Missouri mud and his pale, bloodshot eyes staring at the horizon.

Late that evening I overheard Captain Clark tell Charley that he had spoken too harshly. Captain Clark was the kind of man who could do that.

The talk in camp was that Moses Reed had escaped. There was no question now but that he had deserted. Men had got lost on hunting trips, but nobody had ever been out ten days. Moses was gone for good, and Jack Newman openly cursed himself for not going with him.

"What a noodle!" he groaned. "What a greenhorn!"

"You're as crazy as he is," I said. "Who knows where he'll end up?"

"Who knows where *we'll* end up?" Jack countered. "I could have made it, too."

"You don't know yet if he's made it. George Drewyer could find the track of a butterfly."

"He's gone," Jack said. "Wait and see."

The fact that La Liberté was gone, too, seemed to prove that Jack was right. I asked Charley Floyd about it.

"He did something Captain Lewis can't forgive," Charley said.

"What's that?"

"Desertion is bad enough. But when he left, he stole a rifle with all the shot and powder he'll need for a year. We carried those rifles all the way from Fort Kaskaskia. Before the journey is over, we'll need 'em, every one. Three are already ruined by rust and the blacksmith can't get them to work. Captain Lewis won't forgive him that. He'd as soon lose a man as a rifle."

"Maybe Moses didn't think of that," I said. "I'd never have thought of it."

"Too late now," Charley said.

"If they find him, what'll they do?"

"They'll shoot him," Charley said. "He's a deserter."

Charley gave me a funny look. "Maybe one of us'll have to do it," he added.

I began to wish mightily that Moses would get away. I had never shot anything more than a deer, and I didn't even know whether I could shoot an Indian. I had always figured that I could shoot a man if he was shooting at me. My pa said that you should be ready to give as good as you got. But once I saw those sad, louse-bit chiefs at Council Bluffs, I had begun to wonder whether I could shoot a man, no matter what color he was.

Of course, George Drewyer caught Moses Reed. George appeared out of nowhere and allowed as how Reuben Field and the others were following with Moses Reed. They had also brought along three Oto chiefs who had been off on a hunting party when we were back at Council Bluffs. As for La Liberté, the rest of the Frenchmen would have to pull a little harder at their oars.

Moses looked mighty hangdog, standing between our men. His hair was greasy and tangled, and his eyes were dark holes, as if he hadn't slept for a week. His left eye was twitching and blinking, as if it wouldn't do his bidding. His face was scratched with briars, and one sleeve of his jacket had come loose. You could see his shoulder showing through.

Captain Lewis came striding out, wearing his

blue uniform. He was cool, too cool if you asked me, for underneath you could see that he was hopping mad. His eyes had that dark, flat look they got when things were going badly.

He had to talk to those chiefs first. The men got the mainsail up so that there would be some shade, and Captain Lewis went into his speech. But you could tell his heart wasn't in it. He knew that we had the Oto Indians on our side by now, or at least he knew that they weren't going to give us any trouble, and so in a way he was wasting his time and his medals. He handed them around pretty briskly. You could see that he wanted to get on to the court-martial of Moses Reed. He had been spoiling for it for ten days, and it did look bad for Moses.

We all thought that the chiefs would leave after they got their medals, or at least after they heard one of Captain Lewis's speeches. But on the trip up the Indians had got wind of what had happened to Moses, and they decided to stay around.

Captain Lewis named the people to sit in judgment. I thought it would be just the captains, but he named two sergeants, John Ordway and Nat Pryor, and even a couple of privates. He didn't name me, and I was glad of that.

After much rigmarole, the trial finally started, and Moses got to speak his piece. He came up short, saying only that he was guilty of desertion and he hoped they would be as favorable to him as they

could, consistent with their oaths. If he had stopped
there, he would have had some chance. But Moses
could no more stop talking than he could stop falling halfway down a cliff. He whined on about not
being understood by Captain Lewis.

"You're more than a deserter," Captain Lewis
snapped at him.

Moses gave him a curious look but said nothing
more.

"You're a thief!"

Moses bristled up at that. "I didn't steal nothin',"
he said. His narrow face, usually so red, went white
around the mouth.

"You stole that rifle and shot and powder," Captain Lewis said.

"Why, we all get a rifle," Moses said, a little
lamely. "I couldn't have made out for a day without
a rifle."

"Neither could we," Captain Lewis said. "Those
rifles belong to the expedition. In making off with
one you were not only stealing but putting in danger every member of this party."

Moses looked pretty sheepish at that and said
nothing.

If it had just been up to Captain Lewis, I think
that Moses might have been shot at sunrise. But
Captain Clark met with the court-martial board,
and after much talk, he announced that Moses was
sentenced to run the gauntlet four times. That
sounded pretty light to me, but then we heard the

rest. From now on Moses was not to be considered a member of the party. In the spring he was to be sent back in disgrace to St. Louis with the Frenchmen and the boats.

We all set about collecting our switches. Captain Clark said if we wanted to, we could use the ramrods of our rifles.

I asked Charley Floyd whether I had to hit Moses.

"You either hit him a hard lick with your ramrod," Charley said, "or you take his place. That's the rule in this Army."

We were all lined up and ready when suddenly one of those Oto chiefs came out and started talking at a great rate.

George Drewyer came over to interpret, and explained that the Indians were protesting.

"Tell him that this is the way we discipline the troops," Captain Clark said. "If they could all do what they want, we'd have no Army."

George gave him the message.

The old chief shook his head. He palavered some more, and George explained that no Indian, not even a child, was ever beaten in the presence of others. The disgrace was too great. I wish he had told that to my pa, who was mighty handy with a wagon whip and would wield it with or without anybody looking on.

The old chief added that he understood what

Moses Reed had done, and that he would simply put him to death. That was Oto justice.

"Tell him," Captain Clark said, "that we might have put this man to death. But this is white man's mercy."

The old chief listened to Drewyer. Then he shook his head, as if he had understood but could not approve the justice of the white man. He went back under the awning to watch.

Moses stripped to the waist, and we lined up in two rows. Captain Clark gave the signal and Moses ran through. I pretended to hit him hard but I really only went through the motions. I was scared to death that somebody would see, but everybody was so bent on giving Moses a mighty whack that nobody paid heed to me. I figured, who knows, maybe I'll be stupid enough to get myself in such a mess and somebody will go easy with me.

Some of the men, their eyes narrow slits of hate, used their ramrods and couldn't hide their glee at sinking them into his bare back. You could hear the whish of the air and their grunts as Moses raced by, and you could hear the thud and crack and slap as the whips bit into human flesh. Between runs Reuben Field was chuckling at the damage he'd done.

The last time through Moses's back looked red as raw buffalo meat when you've sliced into it. But he kept on his feet and ran through. He didn't cry, either. His eyes looked red and shallow and his mouth flew open. But he didn't scream. He never made a sound.

That night, when we went to bed, we could hear him in his tent, trying to muffle the groans.

Good Luck Runs Out

The land we were passing through was all fresh and lovely enough to make you catch your breath. Groves of plum trees stood heavy with fruit. Elk and antelope grazed everywhere, and once I saw a herd of buffalo that must have numbered five thousand. The sky was filled with hawks and geese such as we had at home, but ten times as many and twice as plump. Everywhere there were strange birds we never saw on the Ohio. Sudden bursts of scarlet and yellow and purple flashed in the under-brush.

I thought of my pa and his friends back at the Wheeling wharf, talking about the West as their hammers and chisels chunked away. How their eyes would bulge and their mouths drop open if I could just for a moment be there to tell of all the wonders I had seen. It made me ache to want to tell it all.

The only really bad part, except the mosquitoes, was the midsummer heat. The heat out there was like nothing else I ever felt, a heat to make your eyes dazzle and your head throb, to make your tongue bloat until it bade fair to choke you. It was like the back blast off a blacksmith's hearth when the bellows roars. Men were felled with headache as if they had been hit on the forehead with a mallet. They dropped on their hands and knees on the deck or fell forward on their oars, heaving and vomiting.

Captain Lewis didn't take much notice of illness. We had lost too many days to suit him, and he was restless to keep moving. The life in camp made him uneasy. You could watch the pressure building up inside him. He was steady and true when things went wrong. When we finally met the Sioux, Captain Lewis was like a rock. But a broken oar, a burned supper, an overheard word of complaint, were sparks around a powder keg. After the explosion he would just leave, disappear into the forest. A day or two later he would be back, his eyes bright, his brow clear. Then we all knew that for a spell we had clear sailing.

Captain Clark, too, would vanish for a day or two in order to explore, but he would always take somebody along "for company," as he said. And when he got back he would laugh and spin out stories of what he had seen as if they had been stored up as long as he could stand it and now they were just kind of bursting out.

Both our captains were tense after Moses Reed

was court-martialed. We wasted a day on the chiefs from Council Bluffs. They were badgering us for more medals and whiskey, and they wouldn't leave until they had fired the air gun. We finally got rid of them along toward sunset. Captain Lewis called us together.

"You've had your rest," he told us. "Be ready to move at sunrise."

Despite this order, some of the boys went out to the Indian camp to dance. Charley Floyd wanted me to go along, but I was on guard duty.

The night was black, no moon nor stars. I had built up the campfire for both heat and light. The wolves were howling. They made the most eerie sound out there in the prairie, most lonesome and awful, like a lost soul. They didn't come too close, for Captain Lewis's dog, Scannon, was always out there circling. If a wolf got in near camp, Scannon set up a fierce racket.

I was standing by the fire, peering out into the blackness, when I heard somebody thrashing about in the underbrush. It gave me a scare. But I remembered that no Sioux war party would come trampling into camp like a herd of buffalo.

I called out to stop. Then I heard Charley Floyd's voice. He came over to the campfire and slumped to the ground.

"Where you been?" I asked him.

"Dancing at the Indian camp."

His face was wet with sweat even though it was

a cool night, but he wasn't red. He was white as curdled milk.

"What's the matter, Charley? Something wrong?"

Charley rolled over on his side and grabbed his stomach and commenced to groan.

I knelt beside him and felt his head. It was hot as a poker. He pulled up his knees, gave a terrific jerk, and gasped as though he were going to vomit. But nothing came.

"Shall I get Captain Clark?" I said.

He didn't answer but I reckoned I should.

No sooner had I moved the flap of the captain's tent than I heard Captain Clark say, "What's the matter?"

He was awake like a shot and his voice was as clear as noonday.

"It's Hugh McNeal, sir. About Sergeant Floyd. He's mighty sick."

Captain Clark was out of his tent and making for the campfire before I could tell him the trouble.

He bent over Charley, felt his forehead, and then looked into his eyes.

"What you been eating, Charley?" he asked.

"Nothing, Captain. I haven't eaten in three days. My stomach won't hold anything."

"Roll over on your back," the captain said.

Charley did as he was told, but you could tell he was almost ready to faint.

Captain Clark prodded around in his stomach,

and Charley winced and let out a groan he couldn't hold back.

"Probably the bilious colic," Captain Clark said.

I didn't know what that was. It sounded pretty dreadful.

"There's nothing we can do till morning," Captain Clark said. "Let's get him to his tent."

We carried Charley between us. He tried to walk but his knees buckled.

"Sorry," he gasped. His voice sounded as though he were down a well.

Back at the campfire, I could hear him tossing and moaning. After I was relieved from guard duty and in my blankets, I thought I heard Charley scream. But I was dead tired. Perhaps I only dreamed it.

When I climbed out in the morning, the two captains were already up. Charley was mighty sick, but Captain Lewis said we had to move on. The patient would have to ride in the keelboat.

I went over to see Charley. He was lying in the tent. When I bent down to ask him how he was doing, his voice was so low that I couldn't make it out.

The captains gave the order and we set out under a gentle breeze. Charley was as comfortable as we could make him in the stern cabin, but we all knew he was fading. Both our captains tried medicines they had brought along, but nothing would stay on his stomach or in his bowels. At noon he had no pulse and was ghastly white.

I asked Captain Clark whether I could go down to see him.

"Go ahead, Hugh," he said. "Maybe it'll cheer him."

When I got down below, Charley's eyes were closed. It was dark and hot in the cabin and his face was soaked with sweat. The gentle rolling of the boat, which was so pleasant up on deck, was sickening down in that airless hole. I took a damp cloth and wiped his face, and he opened his eyes. He turned his head just a little and his pale eyes gazed at me very wide and clear. I don't think he could see me. His lips moved just a little. As quick as I could, I put my ear down to his mouth. Whatever he said, I missed it. I must have sat there an hour, but he didn't speak again.

Back on deck I noticed how quiet everything was. That day was the longest day of our journey. Up until then I had never realized how jolly we all were, and how noisy. The Frenchmen were always singing and shouting as they pulled on their oars, and our procession up the Missouri River was most loud and bawdy and rackety. But that day everybody spoke in a whisper. Even the birds that always followed in our wake, swooping and cawing off the stern of the keelboat, seemed hushed.

Toward evening Captain Clark came up from the cabin. About every hour he came up to get a breath of air and to see our progress. This time was different. He stood in the stairwell with his hands resting on the deck. He pulled off his hat and ran his fingers through his red hair. I saw him take a deep breath and stare off at the horizon.

He didn't need to say anything. I knew Charley was dead.

I was working at the mainsail, trying to catch what slight breeze there was. Captain Clark came over and put his hand on my shoulder.

"He's gone, Hugh," he said.

I kept looking up at the sail.

"The last words he said were 'I'm going away. I want you to write me a letter.' But he was gone before he could tell me what to say."

I felt the pressure of his hand on my shoulder. "Do you know who he might have written to?" Captain Clark asked.

I shook my head, not trusting my voice.

That night we camped at the mouth of a river, and the captains named it Floyd's River.

We buried Charley on the top of a bluff, with all the honors of war. Pat Gass found a cedar post and carved into it:

SERGEANT CHARLES FLOYD

DIED HERE

20TH AUGUST 1804

When all was ready, we formed ranks and marched up the hill, Captain Clark at the head.

Captain Lewis was already there, standing beside

the open grave. It looked so bleak and bare with the fresh black earth piled beside the hole and the prairie stretching out forever.

Captain Lewis read from the Bible. Then he called out the order, and guns were fired over the grave. It was just at sunset, the sun westering and gilding the sky in gold and scarlet and blue streaks.

The Frenchmen came up for the service, and they stood in a knot, watching. I saw Moses Reed standing among them in disgrace. I had thought that the penalty Captain Lewis meted out to him was too heavy, making him leave the Corps of Discovery. But then I thought of Charley Floyd, loyal and true, dead in that lonesome spot that no one of his family would ever see. I wondered whether they would ever even hear how he died.

We were three months from Wood River Camp and the Mississippi. All the worst was ahead. I wonder if each of us, standing there bareheaded, was thinking it might be his fate to lie far from friends and home, in a shallow grave under that hollow sky.

A Narrow Escape

We elected Patrick Gass to be our sergeant in place of Charley Floyd. Pat was rowdy, but he had fought Indians. The closer we got to them, the happier we were that he was along. Pat needed a cry of alarm, a roll of drums, a whiff of gunpowder, to call out everything that was sound and true in his nature. Ask him whether he was ever scared, and he sank his thick neck lower into his heavy shoulders and furrowed his brow.

"Skeered?" he'd say, and give you a most disgusted look.

Our two captains and Pat Gass could have gone on to the Pacific and on to China and, for that matter, on forever, gone on through floods and ambushes and famines or whatever the wilderness held in store for them. Sometimes I wondered why the rest of us were along, and if it hadn't been a mistake in the planning to take so many. I suspect Captain Lewis came to think so. In a fight with the

Indians we would be useful, but the size of our party slowed us down.

And we were slowing down. The Missouri was getting much narrower and more choked with sandbars and snags. We were lucky if we could make ten miles a day. What was worse, the river began to make great loops and bends. At one place we stepped off the distance at the neck of a great bend and found it about one mile overland. The distance by boat around the bend was thirty miles. It was mighty discouraging to fight currents and rapids for three days to end up a mile from where we had started.

The river wasn't the worst enemy. Along the shore I saw rattlesnakes sunning themselves on the sands. Going down along the shore one night, Captain Lewis heard one rattle in the darkness. If that rattlesnake had known, he would have picked on another member of the party. Guided by the noise, Captain Lewis beat the snake on the head with the butt of his rifle. In the morning we found that snake lying squashed in the middle of trampled grass that looked as though two bull buffaloes had had a fit.

Most of all we wanted to see a grizzly bear. The Indians told us stories of huge beasts nine feet tall that, unlike most wild animals, would attack without being provoked. George Drewyer told a story of seeing Spaniards trying to hunt them with a lasso, and one beast, the rope around him, ambling off, pulling two horses and their riders. Once or twice we saw bear tracks, and they weren't very heartening. They were a foot long and eighteen inches wide.

Worst of all were the mosquitoes, which were as big as wasps and thick as fog. We smeared ourselves with cooking grease, and that helped some but not much. Those mosquitoes seemed to have an unholy urge to jab us to see whether we yelped.

We kept waiting for the Sioux to show themselves. Several times we set the prairie on fire, the sign to come down to the river, but no Indian appeared. Captain Lewis stumbled on a campfire still smoking, but the braves had vanished into the woods.

"They're thirsty for blood," said Pat Gass. "Imps of Hell."

"They'll strike," Reuben Field said. "Give 'em time."

We were sitting around the campfire, trying to thaw out our bones after a day of fierce headwinds and sudden cold squalls of rain. Pat Gass threw a handful of sticks onto the fire and held his hands to the blaze.

"The divils won't pay the price," he said.

"What do you mean?" Reuben asked.

"They don't like to die," Pat said. "No more than us." Pat's beady eyes were bright in the firelight. "Your savage won't attack a strong enemy. It's not his way. He'll try to bamboozle ye. If he sees you're skeered, he'll grind ye like grain."

Pat gleefully slapped his palms together and

rubbed them as if he had some poor coward squeezed between them.

"If he can't bamboozle ye," Pat said, "he'll go into council. He'll try lyin' and cheatin', which comes natural to these heathen."

"Suppose that doesn't work, Pat?" I asked.

"Then he waits," Pat said. "These savages can wait. They've been here since Adam."

Nat Pryor had been listening, standing idly by the fire and whittling shavings into the flames.

"Your Frenchman and your Spaniard gave in too easy," Nat said. "I don't reckon we'll be quite that easy."

Well, the Indians let us wait until mid-September, when finally, high up above the Vermillion River, they appeared.

They seemed to pop out of nowhere. We could be poling up the river, intent on riffles and snags, and suddenly among the trees along the shore were a hundred Indians, chiefs and warriors and boys, standing in a ragged line, watching. They were stout, bold-looking fellows, not like those turkeys at Council Bluffs. Here and there one was armed with an old fowling piece, but mostly they had bows and arrows. The warriors wore leather leggings and moccasins and each had a buffalo robe of a different color decorated with porcupine quills and feathers.

Once we saw the first Sioux, they came out of nowhere like maggots on a dead cat. You'd see something on the shore, a stump or a boulder. Whatever it was, it caught your eye and held it. As you drew closer, you saw with a jolt that it was a Sioux. He was so still, he seemed scarcely to breathe. That was what struck you, how still they were, for when roused they were the terror of the plains.

Both sides were skittish. The chiefs took our gifts and sat smoking their pipes. They knew white men. They had traded with the French for years and they hated them like poison. Even now they were trying to close off the Missouri to the trappers.

We were hopelessly outnumbered. What would we do if the Indians decided to attack? We could never fight them off. How could we fight and travel, burdened with our boat and our supplies? Everything depended on keeping the peace.

Out of the corner of his mouth, Pat Gass muttered, "Look at that thievin', murderin' crew of cutthroats."

We were watching George Drewyer sitting under the sail, trying to interpret one of Captain Lewis's speeches.

"They don't get it," I said to Pat.

The bronze faces were as blank as Missouri mud.

Pat grunted. "They understand blood, the divils. They want our scalps. But there's not one of them brave enough to make the first cut."

We didn't know what they would do next. A sudden shout, a strange gesture, a startled move, and several warriors would leap up and start waving their rifles in the air. Captain Lewis would give them red or white beads and they would throw them in the dirt and stomp on them. After several tries the captain discovered that it was the blue beads that were the powerful medicine. The word had gone upriver that the white man had blue beads. Within a week they were in short supply, but the Indians couldn't understand that. They wanted blue beads. And they wanted an excuse to fight.

In late September we came upon two large camps of Sioux, at least a hundred lodges, and more than a thousand Indians spread out along the shores of two creeks running into the Missouri. That night Captain Clark made a check of the surrounding area and came back into camp looking anxious. He produced arms and powder.

"Be ready for anything," he told us.

The next day two Indians came into camp. They were both chiefs. One, Black Buffalo, we had already heard about as a "good Indian." He was tall, towering over the rest of us, with a tuft of coarse black hair sprouting from the top of his smooth bronze skull. He had black, piercing eyes that met and held yours without flinching. Down his back was a long string of golden eagle feathers.

The other chief was the Partisan, as bloody-handed and evil an Indian as ever drew a bow. One of the Frenchmen knew a story about him. The two chiefs were walking together one day and met a squaw the Partisan had hated for years. Getting furious all over again, he tried to shoot her on the spot. After his rifle had misfired three times, Black Buffalo called a halt. "That is enough," he said. "You can see that the gun does not wish to kill."

When the two chiefs appeared, Captain Lewis tried to have one of his powwows, but it wasn't any use. We couldn't make ourselves understood, or perhaps the Partisan had decided he had something to gain by not understanding us. Anybody could see what was happening. The Indians were ornery and spoiling for a fight. Black Buffalo was trying to help Captain Clark calm them down. The Partisan was bent on stirring them up.

Captain Clark called for the air gun. It always had a good effect. While John Ordway was pumping it up, the captains divided their force. Half went out to the keelboat, which was anchored in the river for safety. Those of us who stayed on shore could see the men throwing up the lids of the lockers to form a breastwork. Quietly Captain Lewis called on men to ready the swivel gun at the stern. Enough iron was stuffed in that barrel to make a crowd of sick Indians.

Captain Clark threw the air gun to his shoulder, took careful aim at a knot on a tree, and sent the pellet home. The Indians ran to the trunk and stood around, jabbering and pointing at the hole. They were awed by the big medicine.

The Partisan, snorting like a bull, shouldered his

way in and demanded to be allowed to fire next. Captain Clark handed him the weapon, and that crazy Indian swung the barrel in the air. We all ducked. The Partisan guffawed, showing a mouthful of black, broken teeth.

The Partisan jerked off a hasty shot that went sailing out over the prairie. He ran to the tree to inspect the trunk, but he had missed by a country mile. We heard him grunting to his braves, and it was clear that he had a low opinion of the air gun. It didn't shoot straight.

Then Captain Clark made a mistake. The Partisan signaled that he wanted whiskey. At first Captain Clark pretended that he didn't understand the sign, but a few more gestures from the Partisan and an ox could have grasped what he meant. So Captain Clark told John Ordway to give each of the chiefs a quarter of a glass of whiskey. John strode off to unlock the stores, but you could tell that he didn't think it was much of an idea.

The Indians were milling and shouting, pushing and shoving around John a good deal more than was necessary. Finally Captain Clark made signs that Black Buffalo and the Partisan were to go out to the keelboat for their whiskey. He herded them into a pirogue and several of us rowed them out. Suddenly, the idea looked a lot better. Maybe we could keep those two chiefs out of mischief.

When he got back to land, the Partisan pretended to be drunk. But even an Indian couldn't get drunk on a quarter of a glass. Captain Lewis had piled presents in the pirogue for the other Indians. The Partisan gave an order and three young warriors seized the cable of the pirogue.

Captain Clark turned to George Drewyer.

"Can you make them understand they're to let go?" he said.

Something in his tone gave the Indians courage. The Partisan, pretending to be drunk, stumbled against Captain Clark.

"You varmint!" Captain Clark yelled, and drew his sword.

Three men — Pat Gass was one of them — at once grabbed their weapons and with Captain Clark formed themselves into a square.

At the same time Captain Lewis, on the keelboat, shouted to everyone to stand ready to fire. He manned the swivel gun himself.

The Sioux warriors pulled their arrows from their quivers and began to string their bows.

I thought all was lost.

At that moment Black Buffalo grabbed the cable of the pirogue. He made gestures that plainly said he intended to hold on.

Captain Clark said a word to his men that I couldn't hear. Then he very calmly took about six steps toward Black Buffalo.

"We will go," he said. "We are warriors and not squaws."

His voice was clear as a bugle.

George Drewyer interpreted in sign language, but he didn't need to. The Indians had understood.

Black Buffalo said with dignity that they were warriors, too. He said his braves would follow us and pick us off one by one.

Before George had done interpreting, Captain Clark laughed. If that should happen, he said, the Great White Father in Washington would bring his great medicine and kill them all, one by one or all at once. It didn't matter.

It was a tense moment and I figured it might be my last.

Captain Clark walked slowly across the clearing. He lifted his sword high and with one stroke cut the cable in front of Black Buffalo's hand. At once several men shoved off for the keelboat.

That was the moment for the Indians to act if they were going to act. But they stood, silently watching, while a dozen of our men, armed with rifles, came back and lined up in a file facing them.

This show of force had its effect.

Black Buffalo whined something about the Indians being poor. He thought that they should be given the pirogue.

Captain Clark pretended not to understand and made signs that we were going to leave. He pointed upstream with his sword.

The Indians only stared.

Seeing the way open at last, Captain Clark

walked over to Black Buffalo and the Partisan and
offered them his hand. Neither would take it.

Back at the keelboat, we made ready to get un-
derway.

"Steady, steady," Captain Lewis murmured.
"Don't let them think we're hurrying to get away
from them."

Nobody spoke but each fell to. We had had a
narrow escape. Nobody believed that we had seen
the last of the Sioux.

❧ 13 ❧
Court-Martial

Although Captain Lewis wouldn't admit it, we all began to see that we would not reach the source of the Missouri before winter. Our slow pace made Captain Lewis jumpy. If a week passed without a chance to harangue the Indians, he would harangue us. He was like a corked kettle with the fire blazing and the steam rising. You looked at him and you knew that something had to give.

One morning we woke up to freezing rain out of the northwest rattling on the tents like drum taps. The Missouri was surging between steep bluffs. No animal would have ventured out of his lair that morning.

Captain Lewis was not daunted. Nothing daunted him. He called us all together and ordered us to go forward. I can see him now, the wind blowing the fringe of his buckskin coat and the rain slanting against his face.

"We're going forward!" he yelled over the storm, his eyes blazing at us.

I looked around the circle of faces gathered there before him. I wondered whether I was the only one who doubted his judgment that morning. If anybody agreed with me, he didn't let it show in his face. Captain Clark, standing a little behind and to the left, never took his eyes off Captain Lewis. Captain Clark's face was, as always, open and trusting. The three sergeants — John Ordway, Nat Pryor, and Pat Gass — only pulled their hats farther down over their ears and got ready to rally their squads. Perhaps old Pat's eyebrows went up just a smidgen, but I couldn't be sure.

That day we fought rain and wind and rapids until daylight deserted us. Our feet were blue and swollen from the freezing water and our hands were raw and bleeding. At sunset we had gained one mile on the Missouri.

The next day was beautiful Indian summer weather, and we could have made that mile before the dew had risen on the grass. By sunset we had made twenty miles.

"You see?" Jack grumbled. "We're in the hands of a lunatic."

I said nothing, but after that day I had to admit that my faith in Captain Lewis was shaken.

"He's a madman," Jack insisted. "If we're all not going to die of hunger or freezing or scalping, we've got to make winter camp."

Jack had reason on his side, for the signs of winter were everywhere. The sky was dark with

great flocks of geese on their southward flight. The
winds, blocked only by an occasional clump of
cedar, whipped over the barren hills. A thick crust
of frost formed on the boats in the hours before
sunrise. Until midmorning the tow ropes stayed
slick and stiff with ice. Even hands toughened
by months of pulling could be sliced by an icy
rope. Such cuts wouldn't heal but stayed sore for
weeks, reopening and deepening. I can still trace
a white scar where my right thumb joins my palm.
In damp weather it always twinges, and I remember the Missouri and the agony of pulling those
ropes.

After so many years it is hard to remember exactly in what order events happened. I believe it
was just after the meeting with Black Buffalo and
the Partisan and just before we settled in for
the winter with the Mandan Indians that Jack
Newman finally fell afoul of Captain Lewis.

Nobody wanted to see it happen, but once it
came, I think we all felt that it was fated. They
were oil and water, those two.

Jack was the only member of the party who
would have anything to do with Moses Reed.
Moses reminded me of a stray dog, mangy and
skulking, snuffling around the edges of the camp
and getting only an occasional kick or cuff. He
never washed, and his long greasy hair hung over
his face. Nor did he bother any longer to sew up
his ripped buckskins.

Moses never said a word to me. When I got in his line of sight, he either smirked or turned away. He did the same with Jack, but Jack befriended him. I couldn't figure out why. Maybe Jack had agreed to desert with Moses and at the last moment thought better of it. Or maybe not. In any event, Moses was always snapping at Jack's heels, taunting him about the treatment he got from Captain Lewis. Jack only listened and shrugged. He seemed to me like a man who owed Moses something, or thought he did.

Neither of our captains was well. Captain Clark had an attack of rheumatism in his neck so bad that he could hardly move. We wrapped heated stones in flannel and applied them to his neck, but that didn't seem to give him much relief. He could hardly walk but he stayed cheerful somehow, and he made fun of how his head was twisted so queerly. Captain Lewis didn't talk. Whatever ailed him, he just got more and more silent.

"He's a madman," Jack kept saying of Captain Lewis.

I had long since given up with Jack on the subject of Captain Lewis, so I didn't even bother to answer. That didn't stop Jack. One day we were by ourselves, trying to repair the rudder of the keelboat, and the rest of the party was on shore making camp for the night. We had beached the boat stern first in soft sand and were standing knee-deep in water.

"Hold it steady!" I said.

Jack gripped the rudder harder. It was too bad that he couldn't hold it in his teeth. That would have shut him up.

"Without Clark we'd all be dead," he said. "Lewis is out of his head most of the time."

"*Steady!*" My hands were in muddy water up to my elbows and nothing was going right. But Jack couldn't keep his mind on the job once he was launched on Captain Lewis.

"You can't tell what he'll do next," he said. "Did you hear about his plan to kill a chief or two?"

"What do you mean?"

"I heard it from Reuben Field. Lewis thought we ought to stir up an old chief, shoot him with the air gun to let the Indians see we mean business."

"I don't believe it."

"I didn't expect you to."

"It doesn't sound like Captain Lewis."

"What *does* sound like him?"

"*That* doesn't."

"Without Clark, Lewis'd do anything."

Suddenly Jack got quiet, too quiet, and I looked up from my work to see why.

Jack was holding the rudder for dear life and staring at it as though it were a riddle his life depended on solving. Behind him on the shore, not thirty feet away, Captain Lewis was watching us. He must have heard us talking. He saw me look over at him, but his face didn't change. He just kept staring.

When Jack and I were done, we waded ashore to where Captain Lewis was still standing. If he knew I was there, he didn't let on. He kept staring at Jack Newman.

"That rudder ought to work now, Captain," I said. "She swings easy."

Captain Lewis took no notice. He just looked at Jack.

Finally, he said, "You're a soldier, are you, Newman?"

Jack looked at him but said nothing.

"Are you?" Captain Lewis said again.

Jack still didn't answer.

Captain Lewis leaned forward, his arms held out from his sides as if they were wired.

"Are you?" he repeated.

Jack just kept looking at him.

"You answer me, Newman, or — "

The sentence hung in the air, unfinished.

Jack moved ever so slightly, really only a twitch, and I couldn't tell whether he had shaken his head. But he didn't say anything.

Captain Lewis took a deep breath.

"All right, Newman. Guard duty. Three nights. It gives a man time to think."

Captain Lewis turned to leave. "Tell Sergeant Gass," he said.

"Tell him yourself," Jack said. "You're the captain."

I couldn't believe my ears. Neither, I think, could Captain Lewis.

"What did you say?" Captain Lewis sounded sort of breathless.

"You heard me," Jack answered.

Captain Lewis said, "You're under arrest, Newman. Report to Sergeant Gass."

That night Jack was tried by court-martial. He was found guilty, was given seventy-five lashes, and like Moses Reed, was dismissed from the Corps of Discovery. He was assigned to work at common labor and ordered to go back with the party to St. Louis in the spring.

Captain Lewis and Captain Clark did something very unusual. They did not serve on the court-martial board. Sergeant Ordway and Sergeant Gass and seven enlisted men brought in the verdict. They had been elected by the men.

Jack never had a chance. Captain Lewis gave his testimony as cool as you please, and it made Jack sound pretty ornery. Then I had to go up. Sergeant Ordway asked me whether what Captain Lewis said was true. I said yes, it was true. And it was. Jack *was* ornery. But somehow I knew that there was more to the story than ever came out at that court-martial.

"Well . . ." I started to say.

"What?" Sergeant Ordway said. "Go ahead. What do you want to say?"

Jack Newman was looking at me hard. So was Captain Lewis.

"Nothing," I said finally. "I got nothing more to say."

That day still sticks with me, rankles me. I have to admit I didn't like Jack Newman, hadn't liked him since we both served at Fort Massac and he spread himself so much about being from Philadelphia. Living with him for a year hadn't made me like him more. He was smarter than any of us, as smart as the captains. I think he might have been too smart for the job we had to do, if you know what I mean.

And yet I couldn't rid myself of the idea that Jack, as cross-grained as he was, wasn't treated quite fair. For some reason I could never quite make out, Captain Lewis had it in for Jack Newman. Jack drew his fire. That court-martial was fair and square. Nobody lied. The story came out, and yet it wasn't the whole story. I'm still not sure what I should have done. But I should have done more than I did. I should have done something.

❧ 14 ❧
Winter at Fort Mandan

By early November we were high up on the Missouri and searching for a place to make winter camp. We had to build a fort that would keep us snug from the weather and safe from the Sioux.

Captain Clark called us together one morning after breakfast. We'd been on the trail for six months, and we looked it. With our breeches and moccasins in tatters and our hair and beards thickly matted, we looked fierce and half wild. No wonder the Indians were leaving us alone.

Captain Clark told us that we were entering the territory of the Mandans, Indians who had settled at the headwaters of the Missouri and who now controlled it.

"We've got to be on good terms with them," Captain Clark said. "We'll give them medals and flags and hats. And if that fails, Captain Lewis will speechify 'em till they cry for mercy."

Everybody laughed at that. We all looked over at Captain Lewis and he grinned.

"These Indians are farmers," Captain Clark said. "If we can just stay friendly, we can trade our trinkets for corn and beans and squash. They even grow tobacco, but it's a mite powerful. When you see a bald enemy of the Mandans, either he's been scalped or he's just chawed some of that tobacco."

He sucked in his cheeks and bugged out his eyes in the most comical way.

Well, we all laughed again. Captain Clark was in one of his frisky moods. When his rheumatism wasn't hurting, that man was a sketch.

The Indian villages we had seen so far were all of teepees, lodges of poles covered with buffalo skins and painted red and white. The Mandans had no need for teepees, since they didn't roam the plains. They dug houses in the ground and then heaped dirt over a frame of timbers for a roof. Those houses could hold several families and their horses and supplies for the winter.

We began to pass deserted Mandan villages. The ruins of those places were most lonely and sad to look at. The timbers of the houses had rotted out and stuck up through the mud roofs like the ribs of a skeleton. Animal bones, bleached white, were strewn everywhere about. There were scraps of cloth and broken earthen bowls and charred sticks and all such filth. Buffalo skulls lay in piles, and here and there the skull of a man or, what was so sad, the skull of a little papoose.

It felt queer to think that a whole tribe of people had lived there and then one morning had just picked up and moved elsewhere. Or maybe the Sioux had fallen on them without mercy and pushed them farther up the river. I wondered what it would be like to live always in fear of those painted warriors sweeping into the villages and howling for blood. How snug and safe I had been in my father's house back on the Ohio and never knew it.

Here and there Indians came down to the shore to stare at us. Finally, at the point where the Knife River meets the Missouri, we found the Mandans, more Indians than any of us had ever seen in one place before. Captain Clark thought that there were at least five thousand of them spread out in five villages. For years they had been trading with the French and the British, so they were well armed with the white man's weapons and powder.

The building of our winter quarters, which we decided to call Fort Mandan, went forward in a hurry. We were, after all, the same men who had built Wood River Camp ten months earlier. The captains came up with a plan for a fort shaped like a wedge of pie. We had everything we needed — small rooms to live in, storerooms, a sentry post, and a palisade that would discourage any Indian who tried to climb over it.

Those four months at Fort Mandan flew by. Up north the days were much shorter than below the

Ohio River. The gates of the fort were opened at sunrise and closed at sunset. We barely seemed to be swinging them out before the sun was reddening in the west. What daylight there was we used to find enough food to keep from starving and enough wood to keep from freezing. When I thought about it, I figured I would have preferred the arrow of a Sioux to starving or freezing. I wasn't keen on trying any of the three.

The Missouri, groaning and sighing in the darkness, was gray as granite and as hard. The cold out there on the plains made your teeth ache deep into your jaw, your toes grow numb, and your finger ends tingle with frostbite. You could feel the cold clutch your ankle like blacksmith's tongs and then shoot pain up your leg till you felt nothing at all below your knees. Every morning Captain Clark would read out the temperature, and there were days in February when it reached fifty below.

The Indians laughed to see us pile on the clothes and pound our arms and stamp our feet. Those Indians no more minded that cold than a catfish minds water. On bright days when the sun glistened on the snow to make your eyes throb and water, those braves would be stark naked, playing some fool game, chasing a ball with a woven basket on the end of a pole.

We hunted as much as we could, often going as far afield as ten days' journey to find buffalo, antelope, or elk. The great problem was getting the meat back to the fort. If a buffalo was shot and didn't have an arrow in it to mark it for a certain brave, anyone could claim it for himself. After sunset the wolves claimed everything, whether it had an arrow in it or not. Nobody was in the mood to dispute with a wolf, particularly after dark.

Despite these hardships, or maybe *because* of them, everybody at Fort Mandan that winter was as jolly as you please. One evening Captain Clark announced that he had calculated the distance we had come from St. Louis — sixteen hundred miles. How we whooped at that! Pat Gass called for whiskey, Captain Lewis obliged, and our cavorting that night in the firelight was as wild and fierce as a Sioux war dance. Even the disgrace of Jack Newman and Moses Reed seemed forgotten. They both worked hard and made themselves useful. I think they hoped that Captain Lewis would relent and not send them home. If they did, they had learned nothing about Captain Lewis in all those months.

In the end they had to go.

And we finally went, too, in April of 1805. The two captains had been talking with the Mandans and with the French and British traders in the neighborhood about what was ahead of us. We knew we could go up the Missouri to its source. After that we only knew that there were high mountains blocking our way to the Pacific Ocean.

The day arrived. Our fleet of vessels consisted

of the two faithful pirogues, now rigged for sailing, and six small canoes we had built with the help of the Mandans. We were, as well, still struggling under the weight of Captain Lewis's *Experiment*. The keelboat, too big for the Upper Missouri, was to return to St. Louis with the escort party of six soldiers. The hold was stocked with souvenirs for President Jefferson. There were cages with a live prairie dog, a sharp-tailed grouse, and several magpies. We had packed pelts and horns and skeletons, Indian wares, and dried plants and seeds.

I never saw Captain Lewis in higher spirits. When the time came to order us to move out, he had the swivel gun fired and waved his hat in the air. The keelboat, looking battered but still seaworthy, swung out into the current and quickly dropped downstream. It was an old tub still, but I had got attached to it, the way you do to a faithful but wind-broke old saddle horse.

We stood on the shore, and the last thing I saw was Jack Newman and Moses Reed pulling on their oars. With those two gone, we had no more trouble among ourselves, and all pulled together. Maybe Captain Lewis knew that those two were wrong for our party and, in a manner of speaking, drove them out. They didn't fit, and he was right to send them back. But I've often thought how hard it must have been to be our leader, and how lonely.

Thirty-two of us were left for the long trek to the Pacific. In addition to the soldiers under Captain Lewis and Captain Clark, George Drewyer was still with us, as mysterious as the day we left Fort Massac.

And we had another interpreter. Living among the Mandans was an old trader named Charbonneau. He was fifty, more or less, a shrunken, sly old codger with lost, weepy eyes and a scraggly beard streaked with gray. The captains agreed to take him along, figuring, I guess, that his knowledge of the tongues of the Western tribes would be worth his keep. Captain Lewis couldn't hide his contempt for this jittery and dull-witted Frenchman, but he amused Captain Clark, who made excuses for him.

Charbonneau brought with him his Shoshone wife, a girl no more than sixteen, named Sacagawea. She was a plain, unsmiling little squaw with dull, sulky eyes. She had been captured in some Indian battle and sold to Charbonneau. Once in a while he'd give her a kick or lash to make her jump. I'd seen slaves treated like that back on the south bank of the Ohio. Those slaves would cry for mercy or call out to their God. Sacagawea, she never flinched. She just looked at him, her face blank as a copper pan.

In February she bore a child, a fat, squawky half-breed that Captain Clark named Pompey.

Sergeant John Ordway, who probably stood higher with Captain Lewis than any other enlisted man, wanted to know why we should carry a squaw and a papoose across the continent.

"She can speak Shoshone," said Captain Lewis, "and you can't, John."

"We've made it this far with Drewyer's sign language," John replied. "We can make it the rest of the way."

"Indians don't go into battle with their wives and children," Captain Lewis said. "This little squaw will show them that we're men of peace."

None of us had thought of that. You had to hand it to Captain Lewis. He was a hard man to serve, but he was smart.

15

Troubles Come in Threes

Sometime late in May I crushed my left hand. Nobody else was to blame. We had gone into camp to dry out the cargo and make repairs. While I was trying to fix a leak in the white pirogue, I fashioned a wood plug, and when it turned stubborn, I gave it a crack. The mallet skidded and smashed my fingers. I lost my thumbnail forever and my left middle finger slants to port — two souvenirs I still have of my journey with Captain Lewis and Captain Clark.

Captain Lewis bound up my hand, which was swollen like a bladder.

"Try to be useful," he told me. But it was clear that I couldn't do much with one hand.

After a day of lolling about camp and feeling sorry for myself, I got restless. My hand was mighty tender, but it made me uneasy to be doing nothing. I asked George Drewyer whether I could go hunting with him.

He nodded in the direction of my bandaged hand.

"What use are you?" he asked.

"I'm no use here," I answered.

He shrugged, but he didn't say no.

The next morning he grunted at me, "You go?"

I nodded and got my rifle.

I felt like a bull buffalo clumping along behind George Drewyer.

"*Silence!*" he hissed at me more than once.

George not only could sight game, he could smell it. He'd be gliding along in his moccasins, his rifle swinging at his side. Suddenly he would stop. It was the most amazing thing to see. He just froze, every muscle tense and his head sort of slanted back, with his nose in the air, sniffing. Then, so slow that you weren't aware that any particular part of him was moving, his rifle came up to his shoulder. I'd turn my eyes in the direction of the muzzle and, sure enough, there was an animal frozen in its tracks, as fascinated as I was by George Drewyer, and living its last moments. My bandaged hand didn't keep me from using my rifle, but I never had to. In the couple of days I hunted with George Drewyer, I never saw him waste a shot.

He seldom missed, and he seldom talked, either. We would stop at a berry patch and hunker down to eat. In the heat of the day George would find a tree, curl up, and take a nap. If we crossed a stream, he would likely as not strip off his clothes and plunge in. I could imitate him if I liked, but he never by word or gesture invited me to follow.

The day I remember best was stormy—soggy clouds streaked with black lashed us with summer rain. We waited out the storm under a tree and then set off again, leting the sun and breeze dry us out. We were on the prairie, skirting a grove of trees, when we heard a great crashing and roaring. It sounded like two bucks battling to the death.

We came to a halt, trying to see what was going on, when out of the woods lurched the biggest animal I ever saw, then or since. He was running at us on all fours, his great head rocking and his fangs bared. About thirty feet from us he stopped, reared up on his back legs, and glared at us, a huge mound of yellow fur towering at least eight feet, with evil burning eyes and claws like pitchforks.

"Grizzly," Drewyer said. To hear him say it, you would have thought it was an old cow wandered out of her pasture.

"Shoot together," Drewyer ordered, and in his slow, deliberate way he began to move his rifle to his shoulder.

I tried to follow, but I was shaking so hard I moved by fits and starts.

"The head," George muttered. "His head . . . or ours!"

The bear towered above us, his chest heaving and his great body swaying.

Drewyer whispered, "Now!"

Both rifles cracked.

The bear rocked gently. A stream of blood shot

out of his neck. That was Drewyer's shot. The bear
brushed a paw across his huge chest as if brushing
off a fly. That was my shot. I didn't think I could
hit the head, so I'd aimed straight for the middle
of the bear. That bear was a big target, but
that shot in the chest didn't bother him worth
mentioning.

The bear didn't charge. Instead, he just bellowed
with anger and surprise. Those great grizzlies were
afraid of nothing in nature. He looked oddly at us,
strange little creatures with our sticks of fire.

George and I were both reloading for dear life,
trying to watch the bear at the same time.

"When he charge," George said, "you go left.
Me right. Go for woods."

Still the bear didn't charge. He stood there, roaring and looking puzzled.

"We get one more shot," George said.

But he was wrong. At that instant the bear let
out a most fearsome roar and came rocking straight
at us.

"Hold!" George shouted.

And then, "Go!"

We cut out in opposite directions, running for
the clump of trees. And it worked. That beast
stopped in his tracks and looked stupidly from one
of us to the other. We didn't wait to see which of us
he would decide to follow.

Drewyer and I reached the woods at the same
time. There was one big tree, and George got there

first. He took a flying leap and grabbed the first branch, swung himself up, and scrambled up that tree as though it were Jacob's Ladder and at the top was Heaven. I was one branch behind him.

We were high as a crow's nest when the bear reached the bottom of the tree. He grabbed it in a great hug and shook it in a rage. But that old tree couldn't be budged.

"Where's your rifle?" Drewyer said.

In the excitement I had dropped it. But somehow Drewyer had got up that tree with his in his arms.

"One shot," he said.

The bear was lumbering around the tree, spouting blood from his neck and bellowing with rage. He stopped, reared up, and raked the bark with his hideous claws. He was peering up among the branches to spot us. You could hear his breath, all wheezing and harsh, and see his eyes, fierce and cunning in his great hairy head.

Drewyer had checked his priming. He wedged himself among the branches, lodged his heels firmly, and rested the barrel in a fork.

He waited until the bear was perfectly still, squinting up into the leaves.

The rifle crashed. The bear stood firm, eyes wide, the blood spreading out slowly across his face.

For a terrible moment I thought that the bear could survive a lead ball in the brain. Then, like a bag of meal tossed onto a wharf, he fell in a heap.

"We go," Drewyer said.

"Are you crazy?" I said. My voice was trembling. "Let's give him an hour or two."

Drewyer laughed. "Stay," he said to me, and started to climb down.

I felt tolerably foolish, so I grabbed hold of a branch to swing down, and let out a yip of pain. My crushed left hand was ripped open, bleeding, and the bandage was hanging from a branch lower down on the tree. In all the commotion I hadn't realized that it was hurt again.

Down on the ground George gave the bear a kick. He was as dead as he would ever be. We figured that bear was a little more than eight feet tall and weighed upwards of a thousand pounds. George got out his knife and cut off the longest talons to take back to camp.

"I guess the captains will want to boil him down for fat," I said.

George shrugged. "Next time you meet bear," he said, "don't drop your gun."

That was advice I figured I could remember.

My hand was slow to heal. If it had been in better shape, the party might have been saved a near disaster. Since we left Fort Mandan, I had been sailing the white pirogue, but now I rode as a passenger in one of the canoes. I think I had come up a little in Captain Lewis's eyes, for everything necessary to the expedition was stored in my pirogue — the journals kept by the captains, books, medicines, and trade goods. Captain Lewis had warned me. "You're carrying the things we can't do without," he said.

George Drewyer was given my job at the helm of the white pirogue until my hand was better. I think that Peter Cruzatte was holding the sail. Old Charbonneau and Sacagawea were passengers.

Charbonneau was the most useless of men. He had spent his life among the Indians and had picked up from them a hatred of toil, a love of boasting, and a tribe of fleas. He was crafty, and he knew a lot more English than he ever let on. A hunter, he never added so much as a rabbit to the larder. A waterman, he couldn't even swim. He treated his little squaw no better than a pack mule.

You couldn't blame George Drewyer for the accident. It was a calm day and we were sailing before a light breeze. The party was getting ready to make camp for the night, and George had waded ashore to look for game for supper. He gave the helm to old Charbonneau. That was George's mistake.

Nobody knew where the wind came from. It blew up, like so many of the storms out there on the plains, from nowhere. In an instant the sky was blue-black and the wind came roaring over the water.

Holding the sail, Peter Cruzatte naturally expected Charbonneau to ease her off. But the old trapper was no better a sailor than he was anything else. Scared out of his wits, he slammed the helm down. The pirogue rolled over on its side, and water poured in over the gunwale.

"Bail! Bail!" Cruzatte shouted at his crew.

From my canoe we could see the men throwing out water with kettles. Our crew was paddling for the shore to save themselves. The waves were kicking up and breaking over the boats.

That rascal Charbonneau dropped to his knees and began to pray. *"Mon Dieu!"* we could hear him cry above the wind. *"Mon Dieu!"* and then a long string of pleading French.

"You fool!" Cruzatte screamed at him. "Grab the rudder!"

Charbonneau only prayed the louder, trying to make God hear above the uproar.

"Grab that rudder or I'll shoot you now!"

Cruzatte had found the Kentucky rifle, always loaded at the ready and lying in the bow of the pirogue. He was pointing it at Charbonneau.

If Charbonneau didn't understand English, he understood the rifle. At that moment he abandoned God and elected to save himself. He leaped up, grabbed the rudder, and brought the swamped pirogue safely into the wind.

From the canoe we could see Sacagawea, calmly sitting in waist-deep water in the stern, collecting the contents of the boat as they floated past, and all the while murmuring words of comfort to her howling papoose.

The day was saved. We learned later that Captain Lewis, watching from the shore, had pulled off his clothes to swim out to the rescue. If Captain Clark had not held him back, he would certainly have drowned in the current and the waves.

Still later, Sergeant Ordway told me that Captain Lewis said, "If McNeal had been handling the sail, this would never have happened."

I treasure those words more than any medal.

16

The Experiment

My damaged hand still meant I was of little use to the Corps of Discovery. Captain Clark looked it over, gently feeling the bones in each finger. That hand was mighty tender.

"What can you do with one hand, Hugh?" he asked me.

"Eat," I said.

"You can do that no-hand." Captain Clark shook his head. "We need every hand now."

That was true. Everyone was needed, for we had arrived at last at the Great Falls of the Missouri.

Captain Lewis saw them first. He was out ahead of the party, as he always was, scouting for the Shoshone. We hadn't seen any Indians since we left the Mandans, but we knew that they were there, knew they were watching and waiting. We had to find them. Once we saw smoke signals on a ridge to the west. Captain Lewis ordered the prairie grass set on fire at once, but no Indians came down to the river.

Captain Lewis heard the falls of the Missouri before he saw them, for the noise carried for seven miles. He burst back into camp with the news.

We all tramped up from our camp to have a look for ourselves. The river was in flood and maybe a mile across. The water plunged and splashed down rock ledges and fountained up out of foaming whirlpools. The late afternoon sun slanting through the great cloud of mist formed a rainbow, a sign of luck, and we needed luck. I've never seen Niagara, but I don't know how it can be grander than the Great Falls of the Missouri River.

Captain Clark said it was awesome to think of all that beauty glittering and thundering in the wilderness for all that time and no eye to behold it. He thought it beat any of the sights in the Old World. None of us had been there to see for ourselves, and neither had Captain Clark, for that matter, but we reckoned he was right.

The arrival at the falls meant we were on the right track, for the Mandans had told us we would come to great waters. You don't know the trouble we had with that pesky river. We'd come rowing and poling to a branch with two channels mingling their waters and offering even-up on which to pick. Choose the wrong way and lose weeks, weeks we couldn't risk losing. We had to reach the mountains before winter set in. Captain Clark asked Charbonneau, but he was no wiser than the rest of us. His little Shoshone squaw only stared. So after all the figuring and scouting ahead, we saw we had taken the right turn every time.

At this point in our journey Captain Lewis decided it was time to try the *Experiment*. Since he had put me in charge of it, I knew everything was as it ought to be. The thing had worried me through two thousand miles of wilderness. Each time we had loaded and unloaded the boxes, I had made sure, and then made sure again, that they were all there.

Of course, nobody on the expedition knew quite what to expect, for Captain Lewis was not the sort to go into detail with Army privates. When the talked turned to navigating the upper reaches of the Missouri, he would shrug off the difficulties.

"Wait for my *Experiment*," he'd say.

"It'd better work," Reuben Field muttered behind his back. "We've lugged it all the way from Pittsburgh."

Captain Lewis's plan had, in fact, become a kind of joke on our journey. When things got especially puzzlesome and we were all brought abruptly to a halt, somebody was sure to suggest as a solution "the experiment." That always raised a laugh. Pat Gass said it once in Captain Lewis's hearing and got away with it.

While the rest of the party got ready to portage around the falls, Captain Lewis took four of us up ahead to assemble the boat. Naturally I was ordered to go along. I can't remember who the others were.

Well, we got that iron frame put together in no time. The plan was clever, and you had to give the credit to Captain Lewis. We fashioned some struts from timber, but that was nothing. When we had her together she was about thirty-six feet long, with a shallow draft, and she did look sleek and saucy.

Captain Lewis was set up by his success. "Well, Hugh, what do you think of her?" he said. Since we had begun working together, he had started to call me by my first name.

I had to admit that she had good lines.

"We'll cover the frame with elk and buffalo skins," he said. "Wait and see. She'll float like a perfect cork."

Captain Lewis stripped off everything but his leather breeches and worked right along with us. We cut and stretched those skins over the iron frame until we had to stop for darkness. It seemed that Captain Lewis couldn't get the craft put together fast enough to suit him. He would step back to admire and laugh out loud at our progress.

When we had her covered and stitched, we had to figure out a way to caulk the seams.

"What do you suggest, Hugh?" Captain Lewis asked me.

"Didn't you bring any tar or pitch?" I asked. I

took it for granted he would have remembered the sealer.

Captain Lewis's face fell. "There must be something we can use," he said.

I couldn't believe my ears. No tar or pitch! Here we were out in the middle of nowhere with this contraption we'd dragged through the wilderness and spent ten precious days putting together, and we had no way to seal her up.

Captain Lewis saw I was flabbergasted.

"There must be something," he repeated, and I saw his eyes get that flat look they had when he thought he was being crossed.

I tried to think fast. I could recollect my pa back at the Wheeling wharf talking about ways to patch a leak. I had heard him talk of pounded charcoal and beeswax and buffalo tallow, but they were used in a tight spot to fill a hole, not to caulk the seams of an entire boat.

I told Captain Lewis that.

"Well, we've got to try it," he said. "Let's get started."

So for three days we cooked up a kettle of the most evil-smelling mess you can imagine. Once it was sticky we tamped it into the seams of that *Experiment*. Captain Lewis pronounced the mixture workable, and he was content. Myself, I gave it half a day at most.

Captain Lewis said we would wait until the

portage was over and all the men could see the launching. He was as fluttery around that boat as a bird about its nest. In the evening he would go down and scrape a little bit of gum off the side of the kettle and smooth and thicken a seam here and there. I thought we ought to have a secret trial just to be sure she would float, and I mentioned it to Capain Lewis. He gave me a disgusted look, so I didn't press the matter.

While we had been at work, the men had been portaging all our supplies around the falls. Pat Gass made wagons, fashioning axles from willow trunks and wheels from cross-sections of a cotton-wood. The men pulled like pack mules, only with considerable more cussing. Captain Clark even rigged up a sail, which helped some. And so, after two weeks of sweat, we were around the Great Falls.

"Now the mountains," said Sergeant Ordway. "At least half will be downhill."

After supper the men gathered down by the water to see the launching. Everybody was easy and laughing, since the portage was over. A dozen men lifted the *Experiment* into the river and she rode high and dry. Captain Clark slapped Captain Lewis on the back, shook his hand, and called for three cheers. Somebody in the crowd — it sounded like Pat Gass — shouted, "Whiskey all around!" and Captain Clark obliged. There was another cheer for that, somewhat louder. Then Captain Lewis

made a little speech all about the problems we had
sewing the skins together and caulking them up.
He praised me up and down, pouring it on pretty
heavy, and somebody yelled, "A whiskey for
Hugh!" So Captain Clark ladled another glass all
around. Then Peter Cruzatte got out his fiddle and
we all danced until we were too tired to stand.

Next morning I woke up and everything was
quiet. Too quiet. Men were moving about like
shadows, starting fires to cook breakfast or getting
ready to break camp. Nobody was talking, and the
air was heavy with gloom.

Reuben Field was boiling water. When I asked
him why everything was so quiet, the sound of my
own voice startled me. He only nodded in the direction of the river. The two captains were standing there with their hands on their hips, talking
with the three sergeants. I pulled on my buckskins
and walked down. Well, it was a dreary sight to
behold. Our proud *Experiment* was awash to the
gunwales, sunk in a foot of Missouri mud. Water
had poured in every seam, and that mean-smelling
caulking had dissolved like sand. One look was all
I needed.

The *Experiment* was a total failure.

When he saw me, Captain Lewis came walking
over. He managed a crooked smile.

"It's my fault," he said. "My fault. I was a fool
to forget about caulking it."

He shook hands with me. "You did your best,

Hugh," he said. "But it's a failure. We won't fuss
with the blamed thing anymore. We've got to get
over these mountains."

Captain Lewis was a proud man. You could see
in his face that he felt he had played the fool before
the whole party. Not that he cared about our opinion. He was beyond that. You see, he couldn't bear
to fail in his own eyes. He took the whole blame
upon himself. None of us dared speak to him. Not
that there was anything that I could think of to say.

Captain Lewis was our leader, a lonely man, a
man too high and too far for us to reach. Now
Captain Clark, he would have slapped his forehead
and rolled his eyes and laughed aloud at his stupid-
ity. And we would have laughed with him and ad-
mired him all the more. Captain Lewis just edged
deeper and deeper down into himself, deeper than
any member of our party, or any party, could ever
reach.

17

The Search for the Shoshone

Before we got to the mountains, we had to find the Shoshone. The Mandans had told us we could get guides from them to lead us over the mountains and horses to carry our supplies. We had brought Charbonneau and his squaw along for just that purpose. The Blackfeet, we knew, had driven the Shoshone up into the foothills of the Rockies. The trouble was, why should they want to come back out to help us? Captain Lewis reminded us that we had seen almost no Indians since we left Fort Mandan. He blamed those Sioux chiefs, Black Buffalo and the Partisan, for our troubles. We had shown them that, unlike the French and British traders, we were white men who would stand and fight. The word must have spread across the prairie that we had big medicine. Now that we needed those Indian braves, they were keeping their distance.

The captains were uneasy. As it turned out, we needed almost all of July to portage around the Great Falls, much longer than we had expected.

The Missouri was getting so narrow and shallow that it was only a matter of miles until we would be aground. Without supplies for another winter, we had to get to the mountains before the passes became blocked with snow. The whole expedition hung in the balance.

So the captains held a council. We had to find those Indians and find them fast. Every day mattered. Since Captain Clark had a tumor on his ankle and could barely hobble around, Captain Lewis said he would set out with a small party and not come back until he found the Shoshone. He chose George Drewyer and John Shields to go along.

John Shields was one of the wonders of the expedition. He was a big, slow-witted man with a long sheep's face and big meaty fingers like sausages. You take a man like Reuben Field, with his long loping stride and his restless air of always moving on. Reuben Field *looked* like an explorer. John Shields, broad and sleepy, looked like a miller. But somehow he could work miracles with those stubby fingers, hammering out tomahawks to trade with the Indians for food or fashioning parts for Kentucky rifles. For two weeks on the trail, Reuben Field was your man. For two years, take John Shields.

Captain Clark said, "Why not take McNeal? He can't do much here."

"He can't do much with me, either," Captain Lewis said.

"He might be useful to carry a message if you find the Indians," Captain Clark said.

The talk was going on in front of me, and I was none too flattered by its direction.

Captain Lewis thought it over. "Get your pack," he ordered. "You're going."

We were off at dawn, the ground still soaked with dew and the sky just pink in the east. Almost at once we found an Indian trail, a dim track of trampled grass leading up toward the mountains. Drewyer knelt down to examine the tracks.

"Horses," he said. "But not soon. Maybe last spring."

That was disappointing, but it was all we had to go on. We followed the trail all morning, but almost before we knew what had happened, it had vanished under our feet.

Then Captain Lewis came up with a plan. He sent George Drewyer and John Shields to each side about a quarter mile as flankers.

"Move stealthily," he told them, "and keep quiet. If you see anything that resembles a trail, the signal will be to lift your hat slowly above the underbrush."

He turned to me. "Hugh, you come with me and keep an eye out."

For two hours we moved slowly ahead. Captain

Lewis never spoke a word. I had begun to think about anything but what we were doing, and my mind was far away.

When I felt a hand grip my arm, I jumped with surprise. Captain Lewis pointed west. About two miles ahead a lone Indian was riding slowly toward us on horseback.

Captain Lewis studied him for a long time through his spyglass.

"That's an elegant horse," he said.

That was so like a Virginian, to go on about horseflesh at such a time.

"I never saw an Indian dressed like that," he said. "He must be a Shoshone."

At last!

When the warrior was about a quarter of a mile away, he caught sight of us and stopped.

Captain Lewis was ready. Sacagawea had taught him the sign used by all the Western Indians for friendship. He pulled a blanket out of his pack and grasped it at two corners. He waved it above his head, then brought it down to earth as if spreading it for guests to sit on. He did it twice more.

The Indian sat like a statue astride his horse.

"Don't they see him?" Captain Lewis muttered.

Drewyer and Shields had come out of the underbrush and were circling out toward the lone Indian.

The Indian had seen them, reined in his horse, and backed up a few yards.

"He thinks I'm trying to distract him while they surround him," Captain Lewis whispered.

Drewyer and Shields were both carrying rifles. They trudged ahead like oxen pulling a plow, searching the ground for a trail.

Captain Lewis was churning with anger.

"Blockheads! Blockheads!" he groaned.

Desperate, he began to rummage in his pack and came up with some beads, a looking glass, and a medal.

He handed me his rifle.

"Cover me," he said. "But keep low. And keep still!"

I did what I was ordered.

Waving his hands in the air to show he was unarmed, Captain Lewis began to walk out toward the warrior, now only about two hundred paces away.

"*Ta-ba-bone!*" he shouted at the perplexed brave. "*Ta-ba-bone!*"

That was Shoshone for "white man." Sacagawea had taught Captain Lewis the word.

The brave looked warily around, as if he thought this was a trick. Who would have thought otherwise?

We were all as bronzed from the sun as any Indian. Captain Lewis pulled up his sleeve to show his arms were white. The Indian must have thought that this was some kind of signal, for he backed his horse several paces.

Drewyer and Shields were both advancing, and the Indian saw his path of escape would soon be cut off. Captain Lewis had no choice but to run a great risk. He called out to Drewyer and Shields to halt.

Drewyer froze in his tracks at the first shout from Lewis. He grasped at a glance what was happening and waited for orders. But good old John Shields kept plodding ahead, as if he were walking in his sleep. Perhaps he was upwind and didn't hear the command.

The Indian was glancing back and forth between Captain Lewis and John Shields, who continued to walk doggedly ahead. Then, as if it had gotten too heavy, John swung his rifle to his other hand. That was all the Indian needed. He whirled that horse around, lashed him with a whip, and galloped off. We stood staring at the wake of dust rising behind him.

Well, Captain Lewis's fuse had been long burning and he went off with a roar. I've heard my pa abuse his hands on the wharf at Wheeling, and he set a standard in such matters, but that was nothing to match the tongue-lashing the captain gave to poor John Shields. John took it pretty well. He was as disappointed as we all were, and he knew that the captain was just letting the air out.

What was the point of talk, his face seemed to say. We had lost the Indian.

Our scouting party had pushed on along the Missouri until now it was only a stream. I looked

ahead and saw a gully where the waters narrowed
to about three feet. I ran ahead to the spot.

"Where are you going, Hugh?" Captain Lewis
shouted after me.

I didn't answer but ran to the gully, turned
around, put one foot solidly on each bank and raised
my hands in the air.

"Thanks be to God!" I shouted. "I have lived to
bestride the mighty Missouri!"

George Drewyer and John Shields looked at me
as though I were crazy.

Captain Lewis threw back his head and laughed
until the tears rolled down his cheeks.

18

An Indian Princess

We finally found the Shoshone; that is, we found two toothless old squaws sitting under a willow tree and gumming away on a few berries. A young woman saw us coming and fled into the brush, but the others were too old to run. They both threw themselves on the ground, wailing, and bent their necks for the stroke of death.

Captain Lewis went up to them, saying, *"Ta-ba-bone."* He held up his white arms, but the old women only moaned the louder.

Captain Lewis began to pull beads and mirrors and paint out of his pack and, bending down, thrust them before the eyes of the old women. Finally one, a cunning old crone, grabbed a mirror and stared into it. She nudged the other one, who stopped her howling long enough to begin to finger the beads. Then the two, eyes wide with wonderment, sat up and began scratching and elbowing one another to scoop up those presents. In their excitement, they almost forgot we were there.

Captain Lewis saw he had won them over, so he kept pulling out necklaces and other trinkets until those old women looked like maypoles.

In the midst of all this, George Drewyer suddenly cried out, "Horses!"

The word wasn't out of his mouth before about sixty Shoshone warriors, armed with bows and arrows, came thundering up on some of the best-looking horses I ever saw. The braves were dripping with battle paint.

I thought we might as well imitate those old squaws. Our time had come. We might as well kneel down and get set for the tomahawk.

But Captain Lewis was as cool as well water. He eyed the chief and pointed to the squaws, who were pulling and tugging at two ends of a blue necklace.

The chief shouted at the squaws. They dropped the necklace in the dirt and slunk off. The chief dismounted, picked up the necklace, and put it around his own neck.

Captain Lewis uttered a few *ta-ba-bone*s to warm up, and then launched into one of his speeches. George Drewyer interpreted in sign language. Captain Lewis told them we were friends and wanted to cross the mountains.

The braves, looking mighty fierce, sat astride their horses. I thought it was all over for us.

The chief walked toward Captain Lewis.

Just as he reached him, he opened his arms and gave the captain one of those big hugs like a grizzly.

The chief was pretty much smeared up with war paint, all red and greasy, and he smelled like a wet dog. But nobody gave that a thought. I grabbed a brave and hung on, hugging and soaking up grease, as though my life depended on it, which it did. I was mighty glad when we could pull off our moccasins and settle down to smoke a peace pipe. Making peace with those Indians was only a mite less trying than making war.

The chief of the Shoshone was a lanky, lean-jawed warrior named Cameahwait, a name that we learned later means He-Who-Never-Walks. He was a noble fellow with bright, knowing eyes. He and his braves had ventured into enemy territory, and they were jittery, at any moment likely to bolt for the shelter of their mountains. To hold them until Captain Clark and Sacagawea could catch up with us, Captain Lewis tried everything. He made his speech, without much effect. He handed out beads and medals, all to no avail. What finally worked was George Drewyer's gun. The second morning he brought in three deer, and those Indians, half starved on a diet of chokeberries, fell on the meat even before it was roasted. Captain Lewis ordered George to go out and search for more, and he set off at once on a Shoshone horse.

At midday, while the braves were scratching their full bellies and yawning, without warning Captain Clark and Sacagawea rode into camp on Shoshone horses. What a story Captain Clark had to tell! Hurrying with Sacagawea in search of us, he saw the squaw, a hundred yards ahead of him, begin to dance for joy before several mounted Indians who had burst out of the underbrush. Turning to Captain Clark, she began sucking her fingers, the sign that she was among her own people. Running up, half in excitement and half in alarm, the captain heard a familiar voice. Astride the best-looking horse, and looking as wild and savage as any Shoshone, sat a grinning George Drewyer.

Well, Captain Clark and Sacagawea got off their horses and we commenced another round of the Shoshone national hug. There was every reason to rejoice. We knew now we could get the horses and the guides we needed to go over the mountains. We knew there would be a river to carry us to the Pacific Ocean, and we figured that there would be a ship anchored somewhere out there, skippered by some Yankee captain, to sail us home.

The Indians seated Captain Clark on a white robe and through his red hair wove six seashells from the Pacific Ocean. The peace pipe was passed around and the great council began. Sacagawea was called to translate. Since Indian women were never allowed in council, the little squaw came in shyly, her blanket pulled around her shoulders and her eyes cast down.

No sooner did that powwow commence than, all at once, Sacagawea let out a scream, ran to Cameahwait, and threw her blanket about him. Amidst all

the hollering and consternation, we finally figured
it out. The chief was Sacagawea's long-lost brother,
and she had returned to the very tribe from which
she had been kidnapped all those years ago. Our
Indian princess sobbed for joy, and even Cameahwait forgot his dignity long enough to wipe his eye
with his knuckle.

To tell the truth, I had always thought of those
Indians as not much different from the animals
out there on the prairie. But this squaw blubbered
over her brother like any of the quality back in
Wheeling or in Pittsburgh. It puzzled me no end.
At night I'd hear her papoose squalling in the
teepee and silently curse it for disturbing my sleep
and curse the captains for bringing that woman
along on an exploring expedition.

Years later, when I was snug in my house and my
boy, Russell, would wake in the night and my wife,
Julie, would climb out of bed to go to him, I'd lie
in the darkness and remember that papoose crying.
And I'd remember that little Indian princess who
loved her boy just as much as Julie and I loved
ours.

Of all the Indians we met, the Shoshone puzzled
me the most. Their enemies, the Blackfeet, had
driven them high into the mountains. They lived
for most of the year with nothing to eat but a few
roots and some dried fish. But they gladly shared
what little they had with us. Unlike the Indians in
the valleys, the Shoshone were always open with

us. Most of all they wanted to be free, and they wanted *you* to be free.

And despite their hardships, they were always cheerful. As poor and lonely and harried as they were, they had discovered a secret. Whatever it is, it will die with their last warrior. I wonder whether the victory of the white man, who will surely hound them and conquer them, will make him as happy as his gallant victims.

❧ 19 ❧

Over the Rockies

From where we were camping we could see the mountains wrapped in late summer haze. They looked scary to me. Even Sergeant Ordway, who had grown up among the White Mountains of New Hampshire, said there was nothing back there to match these. Having lived through what we had, I reckoned we could cross those mountains. We were in high spirits and well fed, we had found the Shoshone, and we were on the right track.

We did cross those mountains. But nothing we had seen, not the Indians or grizzlies or rapids or mosquitoes, had prepared us for what was to come. It was as if that great continent, lying silently in wait and watching us swell with pride, had purposely saved the greatest battle for the last. Only the Rocky Mountains stood between us and our victory.

Among the Shoshone we found a grizzled old warrior to guide us. We could not wrap our Amer-

ican tongues around his name, so we just called him
Old Toby. He was squat and flatfooted. His hair
was cropped off all over, signaling to his tribe that
his wife had recently died. Sacagawea could understand him, but to the rest of us his voice sounded
like pebbles rattling in a cedar bucket.

To get our supplies over the mountains the captains had bartered away knives and guns for about
thirty horses. They were sad little beasts, their ribs
showing through their hides and their backs rubbed
bare by ill use.

George Drewyer shook his head. "Horses no
good," he said.

"You're right," Captain Clark replied. "But up
in those mountains, if they break down we can always eat them."

By early September we were ready to start. We
had to cross a saucer-shaped valley crowded with
spruce and pine and fir. Those trees were the high-
est I ever saw. When we made camp that first night,
the trail was folded in behind us by the hills and
we were landlocked in that valley.

I felt odd. And as I lay in my blankets, it suddenly came to me why I felt so strange. Up until
then I had always lived on the river. Our expedition had been on the kinds of rivers I understood.
Whatever shoals and rapids and falls had been
ahead, they were dangers that I knew and respected.
I had grown up on the Ohio. I knew the rowdy river-

men, the floods and the droughts, the possibility around every bend of excitement and change. The current lapping at the shore was a language I understood.

For the first time in my life I was hemmed in by mountains, and I didn't like them. They were too high and too cold and too quiet for me.

Our party moved forward in single file, and I was given a little sorrel mare to lead. I named her Dolly. She was heavily loaded with trinkets for the Indians.

"These are the last, Hugh," Captain Clark said. He helped me load the bundle onto the mare's back. "We'll need them for the Indians beyond the mountains."

Dolly picked her way gingerly among the stones, her hooves raw and broken from the rocks and pebbles. She gasped and wheezed in my ear and rolled her eyes as if pleading for relief.

"Easy, easy," I whispered to her.

Reuben Field was ahead of me. He started back down the file and gave her a slap on the rump.

"Hump it!" he shouted at her.

"I'll look after her," I said to him sharply.

Reuben glared at me, shrugged, and walked on.

Old Toby somehow stayed on the trail that landslides and fallen timber and mountain streams had done their best to hide from him. A tree blown down across the path meant hours of clearing a way through twisted limbs and dead leaves. Streams thundered over ledges down into gorges. We had no choice but to ford icy currents that snatched at our ankles.

I'd venture slowly out into the stream, holding Dolly's tether. I'd slip on a rock, lose my footing, and plunge waist-deep into the stream, but the little mare braced herself against the current until I was on my feet. Several times we both fell, rolling over in the water, gasping and sputtering, until we washed ashore fifty yards downstream. After one dunking, Dolly came up with a raw and bruised foreleg. She began to limp.

At last we were up above the timber, picking our way along a knife edge that dropped off steeply on both sides. We were high enough so that clouds hid the canyon below.

"It's going to rain," Pat Gass said. "My old wounds are throbbing."

Pat was right. The sky was darkening and the wind came off the peaks, bringing rain behind it. In fifteen minutes it had turned to snow, wet, driving snow that stung our faces and froze on our eyebrows.

Captain Lewis came down the line.

"We'll stop," he shouted above the gale. "Old Toby can't see a thing in this snowstorm. Make ready for a cold night."

That night gave us the first taste of what was to come. We had no shelter, but slept exposed on that high, bare mountainside. There was just enough wood for a single fire, and only a handful of jerky to eat.

I think I would have frozen that night, and many others, if Dolly hadn't been there. I curled up behind her in my blankets, her raw, bleeding back protecting me from the heavy snow that whirled off those peaks.

In the morning the baggage was stiff and frozen. Although several of the horses had wandered off, it was easy to round them up, for their tracks showed clearly in the fresh snow.

I searched for a few leaves for Dolly to eat, since we were up above pasture land. She munched them when I held them out and nuzzled my pockets for more.

There was no more. For that matter, there wasn't much food for the men. We couldn't pack enough on the horses for all, and we had planned to live off the territory. Nobody was to blame. The captains hadn't known what to expect. The snow had driven the elk and deer down the mountain in search of forage. Our hunters returned with noththing but tantalizing tales of a few faint deer tracks. George Drewyer never failed, and he came in with three pheasants, but they couldn't feed thirty hungry men. For water up there we melted snow — in such weather there wasn't much demand for ice water.

Old Toby cared nothing about the weather, and he never seemed to eat. I asked John Shields, who said he, too, had never seen him eat. The old Indian could live anywhere. When the trail disappeared under his feet, his shrewd eye would scan the land in front of us, and he would step along as if he were on a corduroy road. When all was buried in snow, he would study the branches of trees where the packs of Indian horses had rubbed the leaves. He would stop, point ahead, and say something in his gravelly voice. Sacagawea would tell Charbonneau in Shoshone, Charbonneau would tell George Drewyer in French, and George would report to the captains in English.

For terror those mountain passes beat even the Missouri in flood. We'd struggle up the slopes in wet snow, I pulling at Dolly's tether, and somebody, John Shields or Pat Gass, heaving at her rump. The little mare would stagger, fall to her knees, heave back up, and turn her eyes toward me for rescue.

"Leave her alone," I always said to Pat. "She'll get up."

Finally, I was the only one who could get her on her feet.

"Easy! Easy!" I'd whisper, and she'd roll her eyes at me and heave once more. Coughing and panting, she'd slowly struggle to her feet.

At night Dolly would limp over and stand near my bedroll. Somehow I'd manage to save her something to eat. I would crawl into my blankets and fall dead asleep, and in the morning I would find her at my head, blocking the wind and snow that howled now without mercy.

We were very high, and we had run out of food. All I could think of was those summer nights on the Missouri when I had gnawed a few choice morsels off a rib and then thrown the rest to Captain Lewis's dog, Scannon.

Somebody, I think it was Reuben Field, said in front of Captain Lewis that we ought to kill and eat Scannon. The dog had followed us all the way and had more than earned his keep.

Captain Lewis showed his teeth, as if Reuben had made a joke.

But Reuben was in earnest.

"We can eat that dog," he said again. "We're going to starve."

Captain Lewis didn't answer but merely turned his back.

Nobody mentioned the matter again.

When the last sack of corn was eaten, we began to eat the horses. We killed a colt, and the other men ate heartily. Hungry as I was, I somehow had no appetite for that little animal. Those Indian ponies were so loyal that it seemed a betrayal to kill them.

At the low point we ate bear oil and the tallow of twenty candles.

"Eat hearty, lads," Captain Clark said. His eyes were bloodshot and his skin hung loosely on his neck. We all thought that he was secretly returning part of his share of the food.

I didn't know what I'd do if Captain Lewis said that we'd have to kill Dolly. I thought about it as we struggled along. The men had to live. You can't put a horse, a broken-down Indian mare traded for a handful of blue beads, ahead of a soldier on a mission for the President of the United States. And yet I loved that horse. At night when we made camp, Captain Lewis would slowly walk about, looking over each animal. Once he paused in front of me and studied Dolly. I knew he was debating with himself. The men were starving. I was as hungry as I've ever been before or since. He stood with his hands on his hips, the way he always did when he was making up his mind. I was staring at him, and he knew I was, but he didn't meet my gaze. After a moment, he passed on down the line.

Dolly was staggering. I was carrying part of her load, and Pat Gass was carrying even more. In those mountains you struggle up a long ridge, come to the top, and there, stretching out before you, is a dry, stony valley and still one more ridge. Our spirits rose as we climbed up each ridge, only to sink again as we saw, looming ahead, a higher peak.

The morning snow had changed to drenching rain. I was trudging along, sore and bruised, my mind a blank. Suddenly, the tether jerked my arm as if to pull it from my shoulder. I had wrapped it around my palm.

Dolly let out a high, shrieking whinny. She lost her footing, stumbled, and began to slide.

I was pulled over onto my side into the stones and for twenty feet slid on my elbows and belly. The pebbles sprayed up into my face and I felt blood gush into my mouth.

Pat Gass yelled, "Let go! Let go, you fool!"

The tether ripped through my palm and I felt a searing pain. It was my bad hand, still tender and weak. I saw Dolly slide clumsily down the slope for fifty feet. She lodged against a boulder and hung for a desperate moment screaming with pain and fright. She teetered over and plunged, rolling over and over, spewing beads and mirrors and medals down the mountainside.

I lay sprawled out on my stomach with my face in my arms. Up from the valley echoed a distant, terrible thud. Then everything was silent.

Pat Gass came running up.

"Are you all right?" he shouted at me, as if I were on another peak.

Tears were rolling down my face. I tried to stop, but it was no use. I lay with my head in my arms and sobbed.

I heard Captain Lewis softly give the order to stop. We would go no farther that day. Somebody gripped me on the shoulder, and I could hear camp being made around me.

That night the scouts came in and said that the ridge to the south was the last. Beyond it lay a long green valley and the Columbia River, which would carry us to the Pacific Ocean.

We knew now that we would make it. Nothing could stop us. There had been no whiskey for weeks, but the men sang and shouted as if they were drunk.

But somehow I couldn't enter into the joy of it. All I could think of was the high, shrieking whinny of Dolly, plunging and rolling down that barren slope.

The Pacific Ocean

For the third time the Corps of Discovery was building the craft to carry them along a river. Captain Lewis called us together the first morning to divide up the work. Only half the party, however, could be mustered. The men were too sick or too weak from hunger to rise off their blankets. Captain Lewis himself could barely sit in the saddle. Some of the men had fallen by the trail and had to be packed down the last mountain on Indian ponies. We were lucky to come among peaceable Indians, the tribe of the Nez Percé. If they had been hostile, we'd have been easy prey.

George Drewyer, as tough as hickory, had gone off at daylight before even the captains were up. By midmorning he was back with a fat deer. I stuffed myself and, unused to such rich food, got mighty sick. The Nez Percé supplied us with dried salmon and roots, and slowly we recovered our health.

The warmth of the sun, the food, and, most of all, knowing that we were near our goal cured us faster than Captain Clark's pills. In a week we were gliding down water so clear that I could see fish swimming twenty feet below the surface. The country out there was always changing, plains stretching away to highlands or cliffs of rugged black rock towering out over the river. Everywhere the Indians came down to the shore to watch us go by. We smoked a pipe with them, but Captain Lewis made quick work of his speech. We wanted to get to the sea.

How that shore rolled by! Some days we made thirty or forty miles. There were fierce rapids that we would never have risked earlier. We shot them now, gambling our equipment and our lives. The canoes twisted and bucked like wild horses, and we hung on, yipping and whooping for sheer joy. Our passage through that land was headlong. We had seen the wonders of the West. All we wanted now was to come to the end.

One river flowed into the next, each broader and deeper than the last, until we were in the Columbia. We paddled still faster and harder, peering around every bend, our eyes searching for that last blue opening to the ocean.

So fast was our passage that we had little time to get food. Finally, we ate dogs. They ran in wild packs about the Nez Percé villages, and the Indians, who had no use for them, were glad to sell them to us. I have never eaten a dog since. But they tasted good to me out there, and we all believed that they were the most healthful food we ate on the journey.

One afternoon, paddling past a crowd of Indians standing on the bank, Pat Gass let out a yip.

"Looky thar!" he shouted. "Thar! That thar coat!"

Sure enough, an Indian was wearing a blue sailor's jacket, which he could have got only by trading with a white man near the ocean.

After that, we saw new signs every day. I saw a British musket, and the others caught sight of brass teakettles, blue and scarlet cloth, pistols, and tin powder flasks. The Indian jewelry, we noticed, was now made of seashells.

The river opened up until it was a mile or two across. We began to pass Indians canoeing downstream to trade. The water turned salt, and along the shore you could see the tide line.

The final morning was thick with fog. Ordinarily we would have waited, but we were up early and shoving the canoes off a sand beach soon after daybreak. The tide was with us and we were making good time. We were out in the middle, running with the current.

The sun was slanting down through the haze, and slowly the fog began to lift. The light dissolved in ribbons and wisps, and here and there a clear patch gleamed. At first there was only a blue blur ahead, and then, so gradually that you could not at any moment say *There! There it is!* we saw emerge out of the mist the faint line of the horizon. Another moment and the vast, blue, glittering Pacific Ocean was spread out before us in the morning sunshine.

Everybody was shouting and cheering. Paddles waved in the air.

Captain Lewis shot off his pistol.

Captain Clark raised his hand. "Listen!" he called across the water.

Far off we could hear the thunder of the breakers dashing up on the rocky shore.

Am I, Hugh McNeal, the only one among that band who is still alive to remember that day and to record it now? Of all the days of adventure and ordeal that crowded those two years, that day of triumph stands out, the day of days.

We could not know, that November morning, that before us lay great disappointments. The ship we had counted on to take us home never came, through all the months of the sodden, fog-bound winter while we watched and waited. President Jefferson was blamed for that. It was a good thing for him that he did not need our votes. Stretching out before us was the return trip, crossing the terrible Rocky

Mountains, threading the treacherous land of the Blackfeet and the Sioux, descending the perilous Missouri.

We did return. We had other adventures. Yet nothing, nothing in life, will ever match that first sight of the Pacific Ocean. I was twenty years old.

When I got back to Wheeling, I found my father old, crippled, despairing. And so I spent my life here in Wheeling, where I was born, building better craft than ever we sailed and rowed and dragged up the muddy Missouri.

My exploring days were over.

Everyone in these parts knows me. In the tavern on the new wharf, passengers from the river boats seek me out, buy me drinks, and stare at me as if I were a natural wonder, like the Great Falls or the Rocky Mountains.

Captain Meriwether Lewis has been dead these many years, the pistol ball that blew out his brains fired, some say, by his own hand. He lies buried in a grave along the Natchez Trace. And more than a score of years has passed since I heard of the death of Captain William Clark. Word occasionally reached me of his success. He was promoted to general, favored by the government he served so well, given much responsibility for Indian affairs, and ended as governor of the Missouri Territory.

Through all the long years I thought that at least one of the brave souls who shared the journey with me would some day come along the Ohio. How many times I have thrown down my tools and hastened to the river to see a boat slide up against the wharf and wondered whether now, this time, there was aboard a partner of that great adventure, someone to relive those days.

But never once. I never saw one of them again.

Further Reading

Readers who are interested in learning more about the expedition might enjoy the account by John Bakeless, *Lewis and Clark, Partners in Discovery* (New York: Morrow, 1947). Gerald S. Snyder's *In the Footsteps of Lewis and Clark* (Washington, D.C.: National Geographic, 1970) describes the author's retracing of the trail. The volume is enhanced by many drawings and photographs. Readers who pursue the story will eventually want to look into the journals kept by the two captains. The complete text is available in several editions, which may be found in larger libraries. Bernard De Voto published a convenient abridgment, *The Journals of Lewis and Clark* (Boston: Houghton Mifflin, 1953).

Date Due

SEP. 1 9 1991			
AUG. 2 1 1992			
APR. 0 7 1994			
	DISCARDED		